THE
RULE BOOK

'There is nothing yet
contrived by man
by which so much
happiness is produced
as by a good tavern or inn'

— *Samuel Johnson*

ISBN 978-1-326-55293-0

SENNACHIE
PRESS

www.sennachie-press.co.uk

CONTENTS

Foreword 4

Introduction 5

Born in a Storm 7

After the Battle 13

The Sword Bite 17

The Tourist 25

Clear Reasoning 28

The Coffin Road 29

Guidance for Green 33

The Tip-Fair 35

An Artist's Defiant Demise ...36

Waterloo Man 38

Obituary 41

The Will of a Poet 42

The Auction 45

The Cold Room..................48

Jane O'Neill in Court Again...51

Royal Visit 52

A Final Warning 57

Bona Fide Travelling...........58

From Sad Shires 60

Three Years' Bad Luck 61

Lifelong Study 63

Old Dan's Last Brew 64

The Turnpike Sailor 67

Still and Silenced 73

A Bad Throw 74

Fenced Off 74

Calling In the Tabs 75

Official Concern 76

Locating the Lake................77

Fetch the Shotgun 78

A Man Needs His Pub 80

In Plain Sight 81

A Good Plan 82

Returning Hero 83

Welcome to the Family 86

Clark's Leap 90

Ambleside 93 91

End of a Cycle 92

The Wrong Race 93

The Centenarian 95

Hurricanes Down 97

Passing Shadow 99

Bohemian Farewell 101

Getting Better 103

Forgotten John 104

Wainwright's Visit 108

Men Only 109

Mammy Dugdale's Secret ...111

Some for the Road..............112

Steep Climbs, High Seas......114

Ghosts of Mardale Green ...116

Regular Routine 117

The Golden Rule.................119

Historical Note 122

Golden Rule timeline 123

FOREWORD

The old Golden Rule has served the Ambleside community
for generations. Like a village matriarch she has welcomed
customers from near and far, in celebration and in sorrow,
to snuggle up in the warmth of her extended family.

She has encouraged and chastised. She has given and
sometimes taken. But without doubt, she has left an
impression on everyone who passed through her doors,
as the web of time gently falls upon her.

I came to the Rule in 1981, just before Easter, and
I soon found out what a huge responsibility I had inherited.
I have known triumph and tragedy here – and I've
loved every moment of my stewardship.

Martin's book brilliantly captures the times and events
of the Rule's long illustrious life. I hope you enjoy it
as much as a visit to the Rule herself.

John Lockley, landlord,
February 2016

INTRODUCTION

For many years, as often as five or six times a year, my wife and I have escaped from our lives in Glasgow to enjoy some time in Ambleside. The village is wonderful, the Lake District is remarkable – but the Golden Rule is why we come. I don't think we're the only ones who feel that way.

The pub, its staff, its regulars and its history offer rich inspiration to any writer. All of life really is here, and has been since at least 1723, probably longer. In that time the place has established a unique character and attitude, and that's what I've aimed to capture and express.

I'm indebted to landlords John and Margaret Lockley for their assistance and encouragement (especially for one unrepeatable piece of advice John offered when I said people might not like what I wrote...). I'm equally indebted to all my friends on both sides of the bar for their company, their interest and the many stories they've given me.

The Rule Book is dedicated to everyone who cares about the pub as much as I do. But it's particularly dedicated to my dear friend John Wrennall. His pride in preserving the values of a real community environment, and passing them on to the next generation, has been one of my main inspirations. I hope the book helps a little in that task.

Martin Peter Kielty,
February 2016

BORN IN A STORM

Thursday, October 14, 1723

THE ROAD SOUNDED LIKE A RIVER as thick, heavy drops threw themselves into the rushing flood. It seemed as if all the water in Lakeland felt the need to run down the steep Smithy Brow and join the stream of Stock Gill Beck beyond the field below. In the first days of the autumn's heavy weather the road had been rendered brown by mud; but now, weeks later, only a dull grey remained, reflecting the soaked slate and damp thatch of the buildings on either side of the road.

John Benson could hear every drop as he stood at his window, opposite where the path took a steep turn towards Grasmere and finally rid itself of the floodwater. He knew some of the noise was coming from within his home, this once-proud chain of buildings known as Ambleside Hall. He felt as if the rain were falling purely upon him.

Behind him, in the grey gloom that even candles struggled to fight off, Wansted the steward was reaching the end of his recital. 'So, in total, sir...' he said nervously, avoiding even a look at the back of his master, 'In total...the estate is worth—'

'Not even a half of what I paid for it!' Benson shouted, seeming to shake raindrops from every rooftop in the town. 'Damn that man! Damn those Braithwaites! Damn this place!'

His cries drew the attention of two sodden travellers who turned the bend and began navigating the river-like uphill road. But they knew who he was, and could guess why he was angry, and so they made a point of pretending they hadn't heard.

Benson stomped over to the fire and marched up and down as he spoke. 'The land is good. Oh aye, the land is good – but this... ancient wreck of a hall! It would be cheaper to pull it all down and start again than to fix it. Wouldn't it? *Wouldn't it?*'

Wansted nodded. 'By some considerable amount,' he whispered.

'Damn them all!' the master shouted again, his fists opening and closing. But despite that, he knew he could only blame himself. He had bought the hall knowing it was two hundred years old and in need of repair, knowing it was overpriced, knowing the smart London property developer had lied, knowing there was a great risk. He had bought it for one reason alone: to kick the Braithwaites while they were down.

'Well,' he laughed grimly. 'At least it'll be a Benson who wrecks that proud, better-than-thou family's old home! At least it'll be a Benson who brings their hall as low as they've brought themselves!' He turned to the clerk. 'What news of them? When will they be out of Ambleside?'

Wansted coughed dryly.

'Well?'

'The Braithwaites are... are not leaving, sir,' the thin, pale servant said, gripping tightly onto his papers in the hope they would offer some protection. 'A new... A new hall is to be built.'

His master appeared to have no more peaks of anger to climb. 'A new hall! A damned new hall!' he cried in surprise. 'Where?'

Wansted nodded sideways, indicating a point through the wall up the hill. 'On How Head. Stone and slate.' He paused. 'No thatch.'

Benson let out a great cry of rage. 'How Head? Above here? Above... *this?* Looking down! Looking down... again! Damn them – damn them to the darkness!' He stopped dead for a moment, his head bowed, his gaze looking past the fine suit of clothes he wore and seeing all the roughened edges, the hanging threads and the missing buttons that told of a man whose fortune had gone.

Then a new rage built. 'Those bastard Braithwaites have lorded it over this village for more years than God would have allowed. Where did they come from? Nowhere! Then a farm here, a cottage there... and a mill... and then a market... and suddenly they think they're better than all of us! Well, not Benson. Never Benson! Our time is coming – and we'll show them there's a better Ambleside than they could ever dream of!

'But first I'll pull down this relic!' he growled an unpleasant laugh. 'This heathen church to whatever devilry rose them high! I'll take it apart myself! I'll take an axe, and I'll start on that wall! And then the next! And then the next! And the roof will come down on me and I'll cut that away too, and then I'll burn the place with me in it, and I'll come out of the fire and I'll dig up the road with my teeth, and I'll — what the hell do *they* all want?'

His reverie was brought to an end with the realisation that a queue had built up outside his window, and that folk were standing in the rain, silently in a line, all of them looking up the hill but painfully aware of the rant he'd been spitting out with fists raised to the sky.

'Come with me,' Benson growled as he marched towards the door. Wansted followed him through the leaking porch into the road, where the waiting people allowed them to break a hole in their queue, none of them wanting to meet the master's gaze.

'What do they all want?' he cried again, seemingly to no one, looking first down the hill and then up at the row of waiting bodies, who all held kettles, pans and bottles of various shapes and sizes to their chests, as they huddled against the lightening rain.

Seeing that the queue began at one of the doors of his own premises, Benson marched up through the mud, ignoring the unpleasant sensation of wet feet caused by broken old boots. Heads bowed as those who waited realised the identity of the person who grumbled under his breath as he passed; until one fellow, who happened to be standing in the open doorway, was bidden to move his arse or have it moved for him.

Benson elbowed his way into the room – his brewery. There, the centuries-old labours continued regardless of the weather, and of his woes. Thistlethwaite, the manor gamekeeper and brewer when required, was about his business. A small man with grey hair, bright eyes and an irritatingly happy state of mind, he took the villagers' containers and filled them with beer from the taps of a row of casks, laid at a slight angle on a platform against the back wall. Most of the room was taken up with two large copper casks, chained to clamps in the ceiling with fireplaces beneath, while, above the row of casks, there was a raised area where sacks of grain and other ingredients were kept.

'Hello, sir!' Thistlewaite grinned, dancing around the throng of villagers, vats and barrels as he continued his work. 'Nice day again!'

'What the devil is going on?' Benson demanded.

'Making room, sir!' the brewer replied. 'It's time to cask the October ale. So it's time to sell some of our other stock.'

Benson managed to achieve a louder and angrier voice than he'd already delivered. 'You sell my estate's beer – under my very nose? In front of my very face?'

'Of course, sir!' Thistlewaite smiled. 'Does us good, sir. Me, and you!' He spoke without stopping work, serving customer after customer, taking a few coins from each and throwing them cheerily into a wooden box at the end of the row of casks. Through a doorway into the room left and above, a number of hands busied themselves around two large copper vats and sacks of grain.

Benson stood, bewildered, as Wansted rustled through his papers and finally offered one to his master. 'It's one of the most profitable ventures on the estate, sir,' said the steward meekly.

'Best beer in the village, sir,' said one of the locals cautiously. 'We're here whenever you open. Wouldn't drink anything else.'

'Some come for miles,' another told him.

Benson read the figures on the sheet, as Thistlethwaite nodded happily to each villager and sent them on their way with bottles full and purses just a little emptier.

Then the master laughed, a bright noise of relief. 'An alehouse!' He laughed again, this time with more darkness to it. 'The proud Braithwaite mansion... an alehouse!'

'Sir?' Wansted murmured.

'Look at your own numbers! Imagine selling three, four times the amount of beer? We can do that, can't we?' he asked Thistle-thwaite, who only nodded happily as he continued his labours. 'Don't you see? The best beer in Ambleside, on sale to every bobbin-winder, every pig-keeper, every hawker in the Lakes – anyone who cares to cross the doorway of the high and mighty Braithwaite family home! And all because of Benson!'

His laugh was worrying those who stood around him, with more than one deciding they could wait a while to have their kettles filled. But the master could only think of how his family's enemies would react to his idea – and how his father, who'd always called him a pompous idiot, would have to accept he'd struck a powerful blow in a generations-old feud.

He thought of something else. 'Let them build their mansion on How Head!' he bellowed. 'Let them look down on me here! And every time they do, and every time they pass this way to Grasmere, and every time they pass into Ambleside, let them look – and see every peasant in the village, drunk and singing and spewing and fighting… in the drinking den of Ambleside Hall!'

The brewery was empty now, except for Benson, Thistlethwaite and Wansted. The assistants had found quiet work that kept them out of eyesight behind the doorway.

Benson grabbed the thin steward by his shoulders. 'Sell everything,' he barked. 'Sell the lands, the orchard, that stupid bridge and the orchard on the other side. Sell it all! Let the repairs to this house be commissioned. And let there be the best alehouse in the Lakes!'

Wansted stepped back, shocked. 'But, sir!' he said. 'Mr John Benson, of the Bensons, of Ambleside… a *licensed victualler*?' He began thinking about how he might write a letter of application for a position with the Braithwaites.

The master said nothing, considering the situation for a moment, and then reaching a conclusion that set him for ever on a road away from nobility, away from the pretensions of grandeur, away from family feuds, away from petty ambition and short-sighted jealousy.

He looked round the brewery, found a tasting-cup and filled it from a cask of small beer. Damn, it was good, he knew as he tasted it: a soft, golden, warm sensation with a bright, slightly bitter aftertaste that demanded repetition. Thistlewaite offered him a small nod and the hint of a wink.

'Aye, John Benson, licensed victualler.' He thought for another moment then nodded. 'Alehouse keeper – and damn them Braithwaites.' He took another drink and grinned. 'You might say it's my round!'

AFTER THE BATTLE

Saturday, December 18, 1745

NOBODY KNEW HOW OLD Thistlethwaite had become, but his gentle manner and worldly wisdom was more appreciated than ever as he made a point of presenting business as usual. Pots were filled, money taken and pleasantries exchanged as if it were just another ordinary day – and in a way, his behaviour made it feel almost is if that was truly the case.

'They're saying forty of Cumberland's and thirty of Charlie's,' Cookson announced as he returned from a brief visit to the market square.

'Does that mean Charlie's winning?' someone asked.

'Doesn't mean much,' Cookson shrugged, nodding for a fresh drink. 'Doesn't work like that.'

'We'll win it,' a thin man near the fireplace said, his voice wavering with false confidence.

'Who's 'we'?' a young lad demanded from a seat opposite.

Cookson shook his head. 'Idiots. Folk dying and they're talking about winning.'

Jack the tanner rushed in through the front door. 'It's over!' he shouted. 'Cumberland pushed them back. The Jacobites are retreating!' The words were followed by a few victorious cheers, but more sounds of relief and quiet mutterings. Cookson waved for Jack to join him at the bar, where he asked for details.

The Battle of Clifton had ended. It had proved to be nothing more than a skirmish as the Duke of Cumberland took on a few of Bonnie Prince Charlie's rearguard. But the event was far more significant than the action suggested – because it confirmed once and for all that the pretender to the crown of Great Britain was fully in retreat, and the threat of a full-scale battle had evaporated, in

Westmorland at least.

It hadn't seemed that way until very recently. The Jacobite advance through Scotland had been fast and dynamic. Many people who had no interest in putting Charles Edward Stuart on the throne had supported him because they were unhappy with the reign of King George. Others had done so for reasons of local ambition or plain mischief.

The march towards civil war had split families and communities – and nowhere more than in Westmorland. The Jacobites had been generally welcomed on their southward journey earlier in the year, with Bonnie Prince Charlie treated as a hero in the streets of Kendal, Penrith and places nearby. But as the fates turned against him, so did many of his former allies. He'd been attacked by militia in Kendal on his return a few days previously, then repelled in an attempt to re-enter Penrith. His troops had spent the previous night in Shap – and reactions suggested the villagers' welcome wouldn't be forgotten in a hurry.

The door kept swinging as more and more people came in to discuss the news. While most of the recent facts were to be heard at the market square, the important act of interpretation was best done in the pub. Word came of the death-tally being half of the earlier report, of a king's man who'd been captured being returned, unharmed, to his commander with the compliments of Prince Charlie, of continued desertion among Jacobite troops and rumours of rewards to be paid for catching them.

The room still felt tense, ready to snap at any moment – but Thistlethwaite carried on as normal, and each new arrival (for the most part) took their cue from him, and the beginnings of a sense of relief could be detected.

Two young men entered, singing a recently-popularised song about being knee-deep in Scotsmen's blood. Thistlethwaite silenced them: 'If you're going to go on about killing folk, you can drink in the Fox And Goose,' he told them sharply.

Then he laughed and nodded agreement at someone who said: 'Don't matter much who's king, does it? I'll still be shovelling shit off the roads in the morning.'

Another asked: 'What does King George care about us anyway? He's never been here. Wouldn't want him here.'

Thistlethwaite grinned and sad: 'Unless he's buying the beer,' to general approval.

Someone else said: 'It's got to end, mind. You can't have one army going one way, another army going the other, back and forward, with us waiting to find out who wins.'

'They'll wind up walking themselves into a trench between London and Inverness, if they keep on with it.' Thistlethwaite replied. 'We'll be looking down at them: "Who's winning today?"'

All the time he kept his wits about him; noting the lads who were likely to get out of control soon, simply because they didn't know how to accept that they'd been scared; acknowledging the more politically-active regulars in one corner, who'd have to make sure they kept their voices down because others would misunderstand the details of their discussion; glancing towards two heavily-clad men with an air of exhaustion about them, who sat down near the fire, eagerly warming their hands. Underneath his own heavily-clad performance, he knew it was going to be a difficult evening.

The thin man had found himself in conversation with Cookson, saying: 'You've got to show more loyalty, don't you understand?'

Cookson shrugged. 'You tell me what king as will make my life better, and my family's life better, and I'll take an oath to him right now.'

'That's the wrong attitude,' the thin man said. 'You shouldn't wander through life with your hands open like that, expecting something for nothing. The king must lead – but we must follow.'

'Lad, I'm not the one with my hands open,' Cookson replied. 'I'm not the one in a big white house in London, rich beyond rich, getting other people to kill each other in the winter.'

'Ah, what would you know about it?'

'I know enough,' Cookson said strongly. 'I've served, I have. I know what it's like. You can stand here with a drink in your hand talking about kings and loyalty all you like. But you stand in a line, scared shitless, waiting for the enemy to come at you, cold and hungry, hundreds of miles from home, wondering if you'll ever see your wife again, wondering if you'll ever see a morning again... It don't matter what side you're on at that moment, I'll tell you. You go away and learn that, then talk to me about loyalty.'

His words had captured the room – but the thin man didn't want to deal with the point. He stared at Cookson for a moment, then started singing the song about killing Scotsman, without changing his expression.

'That's enough of that,' Thistlethwaite said, taking the pot from the thin man's hand. 'You'll get out – and you'll stay out for a week.'

The other was visibly shocked. 'But —'

'But it'll be two weeks if you don't turn your back now!' the innkeeper bellowed in a tone that few had ever heard him use.

'But... *we won!*'

'Come to me in a week and we'll discuss it,' Thistlethwaite said with a more measured voice, while still clearly in control. 'Go.'

Much of the tension in the pub left with the crestfallen thin man. Those who'd begun to feel that they might be best getting out of the usually-welcoming room realised that things were returning to normal, while those who felt it might be an evening worth livening up recognised that they'd best try the trick elsewhere. Thistle-thwaite was in charge, and everyone would be treated fairly as long as they remembered it was his house.

He returned to work as normal, serving beer, taking money, dropping in and out of conversations, gently guiding them if they needed it. As he took two pots of ale to the tired men at the fire, and accepted two coins in return, he reminded all within hearing distance: 'It's not long since this part of the world were part of Scotland. Might be again, one day. Best keep on everyone's good side, eh?'

As he leaned over to fix the fire, he said slowly and quietly to the tired men: 'Just you sit here and wait till I close up. I'll find you somewhere dry to sleep.'

One of them began to speak in a rough, foreign voice. 'There's nothing to explain,' said Thistlethwaite. 'You're customers, and you're entitled to all the hospitality I can offer. Regardless of who the king might be.'

THE SWORD BITE

Wednesday, June 9, 1756

IT WAS ONE OF THE WARMEST summer fair days anyone could remember. The sun blazed down from a cloudless sky, brightening even the darkest corners in the mills and workshops of Ambleside. The gentle breeze would have taken away the smell of the tanners' works, if they'd been working – but the old tradition of the annual Whitsun week off remained in place. The mills were quiet, the wheels braked and the lades locked; the workshops were closed, their fires and lasts laid by; and instead of the bustle of bodies rushing between the hide airing tents on Loughrigg, there were groups of people sat enjoying the peace and calm.

Not that Ambleside was wrapped in silence. The Whitsuntide fair was at full tilt, with cattlemen guiding their cows to the sale point on the market square, a queue of men from miles around waiting their turn to wrestle for the magistrates, with coins to be won, and children chasing the rabbits that were released from bags, hoping to catch a treat for support.

Peregrine Bertie was a happy man, even if he was a little hot in his robes of office. He felt the joy of the villeins' week off between the main farming seasons, added to the knowledge that he'd been dispensing good and fair justice as leader of the piepowder court.

The original meaning of the word was 'dusty feet,' with the intention of illustrating that the special justiciary court, which only operated on fair days, dealt with the concerns of travelling people who wouldn't normally be in the area when the next magistrate's sitting took place. But Peregrine Bertie took the meaning more seriously, and always made a point of moving around the village while his court was in session.

In Church Street he decided that a tanner who'd been caught using a short yardstick must be sent to jail for a week. At the market square he stated that a disputed horse belonged to one Mr Asplin rather than a Mr Bigland. On North Road he ruled that a young man should be reinstated at Fisherbeck Mill despite having failed to arrive for work on several recent occasions, but that he should be fined the wages, plus a half, that he'd attempted to claim despite not having earned them.

'It *is* going well, is it not?' he beamed benevolently to the four men who acted as his advisors, waving and smiling at the small crowd who followed, waiting their turn to hear his judgements.

'Very well, sir,' William Pearce replied from his right side, the place of honour for a chief advisor. 'And now, if I may, our next point of business is in regard to the theft —'

'*Alleged* theft,' Peregrine Bertie said, en eyebrow cocked and a finger waving.

Pearce smiled. 'Of course, sir! The *alleged* theft of two candlesticks from the Golden Rule Inn.'

'Easily resolved! The work of moments!'

'To you, sir, indeed! But may I suggest that, since the Golden Rule is within footsteps of us, we hear the evidence within? And, perhaps, sample its ale – as additional evidence, if you will?'

Peregrine Bertie clapped his hands together. 'Most suitable!' he cried. 'But small beer only, on a day like this. It is damned warm, and we have much more to do.'

'But of course, sir,' Pearce bowed, leading the way to the front door of the pub. He pushed the door open to reveal a cool, quiet brewing room, well-lit with reflected sunlight from the north and south. And although the sitting room, down two stairs, was a little darker, it was also refreshingly cool.

'Six small beers, Thistlethwaite!' Pearce said to the young man who sat with a group of four by the window, then turned to tell those who followed the judge that they should wait in the room above, while only the members of the court were to enter the sitting room.

'A fine day, sir! A fine day!' Peregrine Bertie smiled at old Thistlethwaite, who sat at the window.

'Always is, your honour!' the aged brewer smiled back, his mischievous eyes as young as they'd always been. 'Are you judging here today?'

'For a brief spell. I trust that meets with your approval?'

'Of course it does! I'm sure even Mr Benson would have approved.'

'Well, I don't know about that,' Peregrine Bertie shivered. 'But he's in God's hands now, what? Or at least, one must hope so!'

'I'm glad you're here,' Thistlethwaite said. 'There's something I've been meaning to show you, sir. I just keep forgetting. Come over to the fireplace, if you would?'

The old man led the judge to the hearth, and gestured towards a deep groove cut into the oak mantle. Peregrine Bertie made a show of looking delighted, then inquisitive, and then, finally, confused. 'Whatever is it?' he asked, shaking his head dramatically.

'That,' said the brewer, 'is a bite mark made by the sword from the Ambleside hoard – before it went missing.'

'The... Ambleside hoard!' Peregrine Bertie stood transfixed. Indeed, so did everyone else, because the treasure of which they spoke had passed quickly into local legend.

'The hoard,' Thistlethwaite began in his best storytelling voice, 'were found in a peat marsh fifteen year ago. A sword, some knives and some arrowheads, all made of bronze... thousands of years ago. No one knows who made them, or why, but they lay in that peat, year upon year, until they were found. Then, almost as soon as they were, they went missing!'

Peregrine Bertie gasped, his hands to his heart. 'No one knows how. Some say it were the fairy folk, wanting their bronze back. Some say it were the ancient king of Cumbria, who couldn't sleep till he had his treasure back. All that's known is, one day the hoard were found – and one day it were gone again.

'But before it went, the sword were brought in here, and that cut you see is a bite mark from that sword, thousands of year old.'

The judge leaned in closer, as if he couldn't believe what he was seeing. Thistlethwaite leaned toward him and said quietly: 'And you know who found the hoard, and who made that bite mark? None other than Peregrine Bertie of Rydal.'

Peregrine Bertie stood upright, shocked. 'Me?'

'No, sir – but he must be a relation, mustn't he? They say he died of a broken heart after the hoard disappeared. But before he did, he made that bite mark there. Peregrine Bertie, sir.'

The judge stood in silence, transfixed, until Thistlethwaite's son returned with pots of ale, assisted by Pearce, who gently led him back to the table and laid a paper before him, between the drinks.

'Our next case, sir – the matter of the candlesticks.'

'Of course,' Peregrine Bertie said distantly. He took a mouthful of ale, then stared back towards the bite mark, then finally gazed down at the paper. 'Bring the parties forth,' he almost whispered. Then, recovering, he repeated in a near-singing voice: 'Bring the parties forth,' He raised his pot and waved his other hand. 'My, but this beer is good!'

Two shame-faced middle-aged men shuffled down the stairs from the brewing room, while young Thistlethwaite, looking sideways at them, positioned himself a little distance away.

'Mr Thistlethwaite, junior, says that these men, Frostick and Hodge —' both bowed towards the judge — 'did in February last steal away with two candlesticks from these premises, in doing so perpetrating the theft of those candlesticks, to his damage.'

'Did they now?' Peregrine Bertie said to no one in particular. 'Did you now?' he said to the two accused.

Frostick cleared his throat. 'It was a misunderstanding, sir,' he said quietly. 'We were travelling through on business, and we had been drinking, see —' Peregrine Bertie made a harrumphing noise — 'and then we went up to our room. In the middle of the night we decided to get moving on to the next place, so up we got, lit our way by candle-light... and forgot to leave the candlesticks when we left. And that's all there is to it, sir.'

'Is that so?' Peregrine Bertie frowned. 'Leaving in the middle of night... that suggests you didn't intend on paying your bill!'

'We had settled before we... got drunk, sir,' Frostick said.

'But they didn't remember that!' young Thistlethwaite said. 'They thought they were nicking out without paying... *and* stealing the candlesticks!'

'Is that the case?' Peregrine Bertie frowned again. The accused muttered that, with their memories roughened by strong drink, they could not say for certain.

'I think we can see the truth of this,' the judge said sternly. 'Do you still have the candlesticks?' The two men revealed that each was holding one behind his back. 'Well, that is repayment in part. You will also pay... tuppence each in penalty to Mr Thistlethwaite. Is that agreed?'

He looked to his advisors, who all nodded firmly, then at young Thistlethwaite, who glanced at his father before nodding too. The accused having also accepted the judgement, an attempt was made to hand over the candlesticks and four pennies with some sense of occasion. The young man found it difficult to make it seem anything more than an awkward piling of objects into his possession – but Peregrine Bertie's manner of sitting on his stool like it was a throne added the missing sense of importance.

'Well, be off then!' he told Frostick and Hodge. 'Unless, of course, you want a drink. In which case I suggest it would be more to your honour if you did business with Mr Thistlethwaite again.'

'They can have a drink on the house,' old Thistlethwaite said from behind. 'And so must you, sir, for your fair judgement!'

'I shouldn't, thank you!' Peregrine Bertie said, swinging round to smile, and making it clear that regardless of whether he should, he was going to. 'But then we should be off. More cases to hear, more dust on our feet!'

Despite his intentions, several more drinks were offered on the house, and gratefully received. And while the young brewer appeared to be disconcerted over the proceedings, his father seemed to be unusually relaxed about them. Perhaps the son might have been more comfortable had he seen the meaningful glances exchanged between the ale-maker and the judge's chief advisor.

'We must go. Thank you, but we must!' Peregrine Bertie insisted, his wavering voice hinting that he was almost certainly right. (It hadn't been the small beer after all.)

'One more case, if you please, sir,' Pearce appealed. 'It also concerns this establishment, so it is fitting.'

'One more, then,' the judge allowed. 'But no more ale. It must be the weather, but it affects me grievously today!'

'Water then,' Pearce nodded. 'While I present the case. Which is between Miss Emelia Heelis and Mr Thistlethwaite himself.'

'Miss Emelia —' Peregrine Bertie spluttered. 'Sir, do not name such a worthy young lady in a place such as this!'

'Nowt wrong with a place such as this!' old Thistlethwaite replied. 'And besides, she owns it!'

'Owns it, you say?' the fine gentleman delivered a performance of being shocked. 'How did such an unseemly thing happen?'

'Allow me, sir,' Pearce said, presenting a paper which Peregrine Bertie gripped as if it were his own death warrant, even though he didn't read a line of it. Instead, he stared as his advisor explained how the complicated terms of John Benson's will had left the pub in trust to his niece, Miss Heelis – who, having no knowledge of brewing, and no desire to learn any, had been advised to close the premises and make something else of the old mansion.

'A terrible thing,' Peregrine Bertie said, shaking his head sadly. 'Such a welcoming place, such an unusual place. Entirely different from those raggle-taggle inns along the road there!' (Everyone knew without anything being said that he referred to the fact that he got no free drinks anywhere else.)

'And yet, sir, there is a median solution,' Pearce told him, at which the judge's face lit up. 'One Mr Holme has expressed an interest in buying the place, offering market rate, on condition that the Mr Thistlethwaites continue to work here – a condition with which both have been pleased to agree.'

'Then, there is no problem!' Peregrine Bertie grinned.

'Only that certain trustees have advised Miss – the owner —' he avoided using her name as the judge's expression warned of change

— 'not to sell, and the trustees find themselves in disagreement. Which is why the case comes to you.'

'And the trustees?'

'I have the honour to be one, sir,' Pearce admitted, a slightly awkward expression on his face. 'And I admit I am of one view. My fellows, though, who may be of another, have deemed not to attend today.'

Peregrine Bertie frowned suspiciously. 'They were told, of course?'

'The laws of piepowder direct the defendants to be present an hour before they are heard,' Pearce said. 'They have not come.'

The judge was still suspicious. He rolled himself round upon his throne and looked at old Thistlethwaite, who offered a respectful, businesslike look in return. He looked to the brewer's son, who stood with his head slightly bowed, unable to hide the tension he felt. He turned to his three other advisers, all of whom decided to take a sip of ale, hiding most of their faces from him.

Peregrine Bertie stood up and moved back to the fireplace. He reached out to the bite mark on the old wood, and stroked it three times with his forefinger. Then, slowly, he turned to Pearce.

'It is my judgement,' he said in a measured tone, 'that the Golden Rule should be sold to Mr Holme at market rate.'

It took a moment for a cheer to rise from the brewing room above; and only then did those in the sitting room join in. Old Thistlethwaite jumped up and shook Peregrine Bertie's hand, refusing to acknowledge his refusal of another drink. Meanwhile, out in the street, the word began to spread that the Rule had been saved.

The regulars from above could no longer wait, and joined those below. Pearce made his way through the throng and shook hands with old Thistlethwaite. 'That were close,' the brewer said. 'How did you do it in the end?'

'I wrote two lawsuits,' the other said, not entirely comfortable with his admission. 'The one he has cites the other trustees as defendants, meaning they should have been here earlier. The one they got... cites them as plaintiffs, meaning they didn't have to be here at all.'

'It's all legal jargon to me,' Thistlethwaite said brightly. 'No one will remember!'

'Especially not him,' Pearce replied. 'He's drunk as a judge! You might as well start thinking about those changes you want Holme to make.'

'Already know them,' the old brewer said. 'No big changes – just more room for people to drink in. This place has got years in it yet.'

'The bite mark was clever. How did you come up with that?'

Thistlethwaite laughed. 'The Ambleside hoard! Them swords were razor-sharp when they came out the peat. Then everyone in town wanted a bite mark. There's one in every house! I don't think the hoard were stolen – I think it just wore away...'

THE TOURIST

Sunday, October 8, 1769

THE MIDDLE-AGED MAN had a permanently forlorn face, although it was easy to suspect he'd spent many years perfecting it. Yet he appeared to be more than content as he sat under the window in the empty tap room, near the fire, with a hearty meal before him.

'Have you anything for me, Young Thistlethwaite?' asked a workman as he entered and moved towards the row of barrels, where the middle-aged brewer attended to his duties.

'I have that, Robin,' he replied, going into the back room and returning with a small packet wrapped in brown paper. 'Is it that thing you've been waiting for?'

'Looks like it. Finally stop that bloody squeaking axle, I hope!' The visitor nodded and left – only to be replaced moments later by a young lad, asking a similar question of Thistlethwaite.

This time, the brewer went to a drawer and drew out a piece of paper. 'Now, your father handed in two ravens' heads and two fox heads, didn't he?' Receiving a nod, he continued: 'So that's four pence a raven, and three shillings a fox —'

'Three shillings and fourpence a fox!' the boy said.

'Aye, alright, alright... just takes longer,' Thistlethwaite smiled. 'Seven shillings and fourpence. Sign here.' The lad marked a cross on the receipt and sped off with the money he'd been given. 'Tell him there's more foxes seen at hilltop!' the brewer called after him.

The next visitor was a woman who deposited a folded note of some description, to be followed by a man who collected one, a woman who delivered a basket of eggs and a lad who left with two copper pots, to be returned the following week.

'You do fair business for a Sunday, innkeeper!' the man in the corner said. 'And yet, you sell no ale?'

'There'll be more of that later,' Thistlethwaite replied. 'These have already bought theirs from me.'

'There's a nice... rhythm... about it,' the visitor nodded. 'There's a pleasing pace – a dance of form... Do you see it?'

'Maybe I do, sir. Although I don't have the words for it.'

'Perhaps I do. Perhaps I will.' The visitor's tone changed. 'Have you a room for the night?'

Thistlethwaite was surprised. 'On your own, sir?'

'Ah.' The other looked doubtful. 'My friends would have me stop at an inn across the bridge there. I can't say it's to my liking.'

'Well, sir, to be honest, if that's not to your liking, I can't say as my rooms will be either. I offer lodgings to working men, coming through on business. There's no call for owt else. I don't think that's your interest, is it?'

'I'm a tourist!' said the visitor. 'I'm touring the Lakelands, looking for inspiration. There is some most inspiring inspiration here – and I'll wager there's more when you're busy.'

'Tourist.' The word was strange. He knew what it meant, of course, and it had been used before; but never in this situation, in this pub, in the sense of business being done. 'Aye, you might well find some inspiration in here. Well, I'll take you up and show you the rooms if you like...'

Thistlethwaite had been right. The tourist did his best to hide his reaction to the basic furnishings, but he clearly came from a world of better ones. He sought to dissolve any potential negative feeling by discussing his excitement at having witnessed the 'jaws of Borrowdale,' the 'unsuspecting paradise of Grasmere' and even the 'pleasant prospect of Ambleside itself ' – and Thistlethwaite appreciated the gesture.

As the pair arrived at the foot of the stairway, the front door opened to herald the arrival of the Reverend John Wilson of Grasmere. 'My dear Mr Gray – have you been here all this time? We missed you!' cried the clergyman.

The tourist nodded. 'I came seeking inspiration, Reverend Wilson. And I dare say I found it. I should like to stop in Ambleside tonight, although not in that other place... and not here, I'm afraid.' He smiled at the brewer, who acknowledged the politeness.

'Stop in Ambleside? I don't think so...' the vicar said dismissively. 'No, sir, we must push on! You'll find no ivy-mantled towers in this place!'

Old Danny pushed his way past Wilson and settled in his usual seat near the fire, nodding for a pot of small beer, which gave him an excuse to be out of his house for a while. He waited patiently as the visitor settled his bill while the vicar badgered around him then hastened his departure. Finally Thistlethwaite brought over two pots of ale and sat down too.

'That were Mr Thomas Gray,' Danny said.

'He said he were a tourist.'

'He is that – he's writing a journal of his travels around the Lakes. I reckon you'll see it published in a year or two.'

'Is that what them tourists do? Write journals? I've often wondered. What makes them think they'll be published?'

'Some will pay for it themselves – if you can afford to travel round without work, you can afford that,' said Danny, taking a drink. 'But that one, he'll be paid to his, he will.'

'How's that?'

'Because that were Mr Thomas Gray, who published his *Elegy Written In A Country Churchyard*.' He began reciting the poem quietly to himself. 'The curfew tolls the knell of parting day, the lowing herd wind slowly o'er the lea...'

'Tourism,' Thistlethwaite said into his pot. 'It'll never catch on.'

CLEAR REASONING

Saturday, August 2, 1777

Dear Sirs —

I am forced to contest Mr Benson's recent claim in these pages that I, the owner of the Golden Rule Inn, Ambleside, attempted to mislead him as he discharged his duty as Assessor of the Window Tax.

Mr Benson and his Collector, Mr Partridge, were both made welcome at my premises and enjoyed the fine work of my innkeeper, Mr Thistlethwaite, and his son, and expressed themselves happy with their visit.

There was no need for Mr Benson to suggest, as he has done, that I laboured to conceal the true number of windows in the building, in order to pay less tax than I must.

Your readers will recollect that it would have been a fruitless effort, since the building once belonged to Mr Benson's late father, and he himself spent many years within its walls as a young man.

I find myself of the conclusion that Mr Benson miscounted the windows, and felt the need to blame another. That failing in numbers may, I also conclude, be one of the reasons why I now own the Golden Rule, and his family does not.

Yours etc

William Holme, Ambleside

THE COFFIN ROAD

Thursday, February 5, 1784

I'll wring his neck, even if I do hang for it. I'll drop him off the bridge. He'll regret it till his dying day – if he lives that long.

Don't go on about it. You don't know what's going on out there. It's terrible weather.

Weather's got nothing to do with it. He's away drinking some-where. And you'd think drinking in here every day would be enough for him.

I'm just saying, you'll regret it if something's happened to him.

He'll be the one regretting. That he will.

They say fifty sheep were buried in snow at Eden, and had to be dug out a week later. They survived, mind.

He won't.

And I heard a big boulder cracked with the cold and rolled down hill at Beetham.

He'll wish it had landed on him.

And Derwentwater is frozen so deep that you can walk out to the islands.

I'll walk all over him when I see him.

Don't go on about it. You never know —

— Ah, what a surprise, there he is! Straight into the Rule, if you please. And what will be your story this time?

Oh, love, the day I've had.

The *three* days you've had.

Is it? Aye, I suppose it is. Been terrible, so it has. Wait till I get myself a drink and I'll tell you.

I'm wagering it won't be your first today. Did you go home first to see if I were there, or did you just come straight here?

It's the first stop, love – I'm just back from Grasmere.

Grasmere? That's a new one. Go on, then, tell us, why were you in Grasmere?

Well, the other night, old Joe Heaton's brother came to see me. You'll remember as Joe died of the cold?

Hmm. What about it?

Well, Joe's brother said he were in trouble with the vicar at Grasmere, on account of not having had Joe buried. And, of course, because Joe were born above stock, he has to go

to Grasmere to be buried. In this weather!

That's cozy, isn't it?

You can't blame me, love – I've said for years they need to let us bury folk from above stock at the church here, instead of making us go all those miles on the coffin road. With a blizzard blowing an'all!

Aye, well…

So we got the lads together and got Joe's coffin on the cart, and we started off for Grasmere. It were terrible, up on them hills in that snow —–

— Why didn't you take the turnpike?

You can't blame me, love – you know Joe weren't made of money. We couldn't pay the toll for him and his cart and his brother, could we?

Couldn't you…

Aye, but then Joe's brother slipped on ice and went down the hill, and broke his leg! Took an hour to get him back up again. We had to sit him on top of Joe's coffin, and with one less to help it took longer. Took us six hours, in all, I reckon.

So that's six hours, out of three days.

Aye, but then, when we got to Grasmere church, there was business being done in the west porch, and the vicar wouldn't stop it. So that were another delay.

What, another hour?

Aye, but then, the gravediggers took their time getting the snow out of their hole, so we could put Joe in it. It were night-time by then. You can't take the coffin road home by night, can you? Unless you want to end up in one yourself.

Alright. So that's a day.

Aye, but then, there were nowhere for us to stop, with the

inn full and Joe's brother living in a tiny little place. We wound up in the poor house!

So?

Well, we didn't have pauper badges, did we, because we're not paupers. But the warden, he says we're to be punished for not observing rules – so after we're up in the morning, he puts us in the dungeon!

I thought it were four hours in there for not wearing a pauper's badge?

Aye, but then when he came to let us out, the door were frozen with the cold. Took them all day to get it free, as they fed us bits and bobs through the bars. Then when they got it open, it were too late to come home again.

So you should have been back yesterday.

Aye, but then we came back along turnpike, because there were too much snow on coffin road. The road at Brathay Bridge were like a sheet of ice – we couldn't get over it.

There's plenty of people came from Brathay yesterday.

Not with a cart, though. You can't blame me, love – I've said since they finished rebuilding bridge that they'd done it wrong and it would be no good in winter. And a winter like this...

That doesn't explain why you didn't come back last night.

Aye, but after sitting all day we thought we'd best go back if we couldn't go forward. When Joe's brother saw us giving up on going home, two days after we'd done him a favour, he said it were only right to give us a supper.

You could have come home after that.

Aye, but then, after the days I'd had, the beer went right to my head. I just had to sleep. You can't blame me, love – you know how I get if I don't have beer every day. So they let me

sleep till midday, because I needed it. And then we came home.

It doesn't take seven hours on the turnpike. Even in this weather.

Aye, but then the turnpike were blocked with the fresh snow. We had to go back and leave the cart at Grasmere church. You can't blame me, love – I've said for years there's parts of that road as need better looking after in winter...

So is that it? Are you finished?

Aye, that's it, love. That's enough, innit? Oh, I could do with another drink now, Hold on...

Are you going to let him away with that?

You just told me to go easy on him!

That was before he gave you all that rubbish!

It were a good one, though, weren't it? Best he's come up with in years...

GUIDANCE FOR GREEN

Monday, April 22, 1793

THISTLETHWAITE WAS BECOMING EXASPERATED. He didn't like feeling that way, especially as his father and grandfather before him had always made a point of never becoming exasperated at the behaviour of customers, it being against the spirit of good inn-keeping. He wished he had their fortitude – but he didn't.

'My guide book will change everything!' William Green insisted, gesturing towards the sketches and reports he'd laid on the table before the landlord.

'It may, and it may not,' Thistlethwaite replied. 'But I've told you before, I'm not interested.'

'Ambleside has been so slow to take advantage of the tourist trade. But I'll change that – and you need to be part of it.'

'I think I'll decide what I need to be part of, and what I don't.'

'Look!' Green read from one of the papers. 'Ambleside is the bustling home of eighteen mills, with a geography reminiscent of the Alps of Switzerland.' He pointed to a sketch. 'With that text placed beside that scene, the contrast will be so convincing, we'll have people packing to leave in minutes!'

The other shook his head. 'This is a simple country inn,' he said. 'If people want to come in, have a drink, and have a talk, they're welcome. If they don't, they're not. I have no need to advertise my business. Those who need it know about it.'

'But what about competition? The other inns have all signed up. You'll be the only one left out.'

'So be it.'

'Think about it,' Green persisted, grabbing Thistlethwaite's arm. 'My paintings are doing well. My guide will do better. Ambleside will benefit from my work and you'd be a fool to miss out.'

Thistlethwaite pushed the artist's arm away. 'Mr Green, you're not from here so you wouldn't know this, but there's Ambleside, and then there's the Golden Rule. This is a place where people come to get away from the rest of the village. That's what it's here for. And to be plain, Mr Green, the more you shout about the rest of Ambleside to people from London like yourself, the more others will need the Golden Rule.'

Green glared with a look somewhere between confusion and fury. 'You need me more than I need you,' he said tersely.

'No, I don't. But I'll tell you what – plenty of folk who see your nice paintings and read your fine words will come up here, realise it's not all what you've said it is, and maybe find themselves in here with me and my regulars. And they'll be welcome, each and every one of them. So would you be... if you only respected that you're a guest in someone else's house.'

Thistlethwaite knew he was probably over-reacting. There was no doubting the quality of Green's work. But it seemed that the artist wasn't used to being refused, and that lent an attitude to him that the landlord didn't like. Which was the main reason he wanted to say 'no' – and had done.

Green made a dismissive noise and turned to leave. But he turned back again. 'I think you should know what I'm going to write,' he hissed. 'I'm going to say, 'Ambleside is serviced by five inns, of varying character: the Salutation, the Commercial, the White Lion, the Fox And Goose... and one unsigned'.'

Thistlethwaite sighed. 'The sign is being repainted – it'll be back tomorrow.'

'That's just terrible bad luck for you, isn't it?' Green said with an unpleasant grin as he marched out.

'I don't think so,' the landlord said to his back.

THE TIP-FAIR

Saturday, November 2, 1793

Dear Sirs —

*I wish to bear witness to the truth of a phrase
that has been heard on the streets of Ambleside.
It is said that October's annual 'Tip-Fair' is viewed
with little seriousness by those who are expected
to undertake cattle transactions at Market Square,
and instead, for them, 'The Tip-Fair begins at
mid-day and ends at noon.'*

This does indeed seem to be the case;
and, worse, I believe that several dealers
do not even travel as far as Market Square,
but rather agree the details of their transactions
on the road, then celebrate each others'
good fortune at the Golden Rule Inn.

This behaviour is to be regretted.

Yours sincerely
Name Withheld

AN ARTIST'S DEFIANT DEMISE

Friday, August 2, 1805

Well, they found that artist then.

What artist?

Gough. Him that went missing on Helvellyn in spring.

Oh aye. Dead, then, is he?

Aye. All they found were his skeleton, and a couple of them painting mirrors, and his hat. It were torn in two, so they reckon he fell off Striding Edge.

You will do, if you go up there at the beginning of the year.

Alone an' all.

Pillock.

He'd arranged to be guided by Eddie Asplin, you see, but Eddie had to work.

He'd have been alright if he'd gone up with Asplin.

But he didn't, so he wasn't.

That'll learn him.

They found his dog with him.

Dead an'all?

No – very much alive. It had a pup, but pup died.

Suppose it would, in that weather, up there for that time.

They say Gough's body had been eaten away to the bone.

Must have been the dog.

No, they say it were ravens.

It will have been the bloody dog. What else it is meant to do?

Well, it stayed up there with him, so it must have been loyal.

Loyal's one thing. Staying alive is another.

Aye. But the paper's saying he died an artist's death, up on the tops looking for inspiration.

Oh, bloody 'ell.

Aye. So doubtless there'll be more artists coming by, to shed a tear and paint a picture about his defiant demise or whatnot.

Well, they've every right, I suppose.

Happen they may have. But what gets me is when they move a river here, change a top there, and all that. The next year you have folk coming up, looking for the scene of the picture – and you need to tell them it's not there!

Spoils it for me an'all. But I suppose all that art's not for us.

Bloody should be, though.

Aye. Shall we have a drink to old Gough then?

Why not.

WATERLOO MAN

Wednesday, January 15, 1817

SERGEANT THOMAS DUGDALE needed no introduction, and nor did he need to place an order for a drink, because his preference was known. Instead, Thistlethwaite filled a pot from the barrel beside him and held it out for the tall, thin man, who'd just arrived with a throng of younger men behind him, and a wisp of cold air from the winter's day beyond. 'It's on the house,' the innkeeper told the near-dozen people who offered to pay for the ale.

Silence fell as all in the busy taproom watched him drink, then grin, then salute the brewer. 'Fine as ever, Frank!' he said.

'Welcome back, Tom,' Thistlethwaite replied.

Near the fire, old Danny was recounting Dugdale's history for its own sake, since everyone knew it. 'Captured a French general at Waterloo – and that after he'd had his horse shot from under him with cannon fire. Then he rescued a Prussian patrol and led them onto the field just in time to make Bony turn his back! Look, there's his medal.'

Despite themselves, everyone in the right position craned to look at the silver disc pinned to Dugdale's jacket. 'The Waterloo Medal,' old Danny said. 'With his name inscribed around edge. They gave him two years with pay on his service record!'

Walter Bigland came up from the sitting room, having detected the change of mood in the taproom. 'Our guest has arrived!' he said, shaking Dugdale's hand.

'That I have,' said the soldier. 'But I don't rightly know what you want of me.'

'Not much,' Bigland grinned, leading him down the stairs as the rest of the room watched. 'We just hope you can help us with a little problem.'

Dugdale sat nearest the fire, the place of honour, while Bigland explained. 'These men you see here are some of the members of the Ambleside Bond for the Prosecution of Felons.' He offered a hand-bill containing further information. 'We sit, once a year, in place of the magistrate, who can't be here during the bad weather of winter. We dispense justice in the interests of the parish – for no pay, mind, only a supper afterwards.'

'I've heard there's many of them bonds starting up these last few years,' Dugdale said, realising that, yet again, people expected him to say things, regardless of whether he had any opinion.

'It's a difficult time,' Bigland replied. 'Now the war's over there's many a man coming home – with not as much as you to show for it. We have to protect the parish.'

'And what can I do?'

'All we ask is that you sit through the hearings with us today, then join us for supper.'

Dugdale looked round. It was one of the least demanding tasks he'd been given since arriving home as a hero. In fact, the idea of simply sitting down and drinking Golden Rule ale appealed to him immensely. He resented the idea that such simple luxuries might be beyond him for ever, due to the attention turned on him just because he'd been doing his duty. 'I can do that!' he smiled.

The bond members murmured their thanks. 'Having a Waterloo Man among us will make things easier than they were last year,' Bigland said.

'Why? What happened last year?'

The other rolled his eyes. 'Oh, every felon of any size admitted their crime, but then asked for leniency on account of we'd won at Waterloo. And many of the bond, not us, were minded to grant it. So as a result, the number of felons we'll be dealing with this year is near double what it usually is – and most of them are those as got leniency last year!'

Dugdale laughed. 'And having me among you will shut them up this time?'

'We hope so!'

'Aye, I'll be glad to,' said the soldier. 'I'll get myself another drink, then you can tell me where we're going.'

'Allow me,' said the bondsmen all together.

'If you don't mind,' he smiled at them, 'I'll get it myself. Reminds me of the old days, when I were just Tom Dugdale who sat in the corner.' He moved past the men and went up the stairs, tapping Thistlethwaite on the shoulder and gesturing towards his empty pot.

'On the house again,' the brewer told him, winking one of his bright eyes.

But the soldier held up a coin. 'Frank, I'm just me, just a soldier, and I want to buy myself a drink. Is that alright?'

'Of course it is. Might as well buy me one!'

Another pot filled, the pair clashed them together and drank, while the taproom got on with its business, unaware that Dugdale had come up from the sitting room. 'What are your plans, Tom?' Thistlethwaite asked.

'Well, I reckon there's only one way I'll get peace and quiet to enjoy my drinking,' Dugdale said. 'I reckon I'll get myself a pub.'

'Well not in bloody Ambleside,' the brewer said quickly. 'All my regulars will be round yours like a shot, to drink with a hero. I've taken into partnership with young Will Wilson – I'd have to let him go again. What would I have left?'

'Better beer, and a better welcome, probably,' Dugdale replied, laughing. 'But don't worry – I'll settle somewhere else. Is Penrith far enough?'

'Suppose that'll do,' said Thistlethwaite.

OBITUARY

Saturday, July 6, 1822

By special request the following obituary is printed although somewhat belated. It was read at the deceased's funeral service at Grasmere by Rector Richard Fleming.

This service is held in memory of Francis Thistlethwaite, who was born September 29, 1757 and died June 14, 1822 at the age of 65 years, 9 months and 15 days.

His passing marks the end of 99 years' service in hospitality by three generations of Thistlethwaites, who operated the Golden Rule Inn at Ambleside.

Francis, son of Francis, son of John, was highly-regarded as a leading member of the community, thought of by many as a beneficial host, teacher and advisor.

It was said of him that he learned from the experiences of all those who visited his hostelry, and reflected those lessons in his own life, and therefore those of his customers.

Although illness prevented the achievement of his ambition to complete a century of service by the Thistlethwaites, he found time in his final years to instruct Mr William Wilson in the arts and manners of good innkeeping.

Mr Wilson hereby vows to do his best to reach the high standards set by him, his father and his grandfather, in the spirit of the original 'Golden Rule' – do unto others as you would have done unto you.

He further vows to ensure the future of the inn for at least a century to come.

THE WILL OF A POET

Thursday, September 25, 1823

'DEAR WILL! It is our Will! If it is your will!' said Hartley Coleridge, his arms open in appeal across the bar, from where William Wilson regarded him with an even glance. 'Our protector, our preserver – our preserver, if you will, Will!'

Coleridge stared hopefully towards the back room; and, finally, sighing dramatically, Wilson went to the row of tapped barrels and returned with two pots of ale.

'Our preserver preserves!' said Coleridge as he gratefully grasped his drink in both hands. 'And we thank him for his will in the matter, do we not, Tom?'

Thomas De Quincey's hands were on his head, his elbows on the bar. 'The affrontery!' he muttered, shaking his torso from side to side. 'They threw... stones at us, Will! They threw stones at us!'

'Did they really,' Wilson replied evenly.

'At the finest editor the Westmorland Gazette ever had – and could not keep!' said Coleridge, nodding towards his friend before taking a long drink. 'This is the good stuff, is it not? It's not the small beer?' He was ignored.

'Stones at the finest literary critic of his generation!' De Quincey said in support of his companion.

'The way I hear it,' Wilson replied, 'You were throwing stones at the schoolboys.'

'Never!'

'Because they laughed at you.'

'At us!'

'Because you fell on your arses as you came out the Unicorn.'

'The Unicorn!' De Quincey shouted. 'Us? In there? We would

never...'

Coleridge waved a finger in the manner of a schoolteacher – which he was. 'When things like that can be said about things like us... people like us... well, it's time for change. Change!' He leaned towards the innkeeper. 'Like when his mother changed their name,' he whispered. 'De Quincey. Do you know what his name was before that?'

'Quincey,' Wilson said flatly.

'Quincey!' nodded Coleridge smugly. 'And yet he scorns all to do with the French. Why, only last month he wrote in the —'

'Silence, I pray!' his friend called, throwing his arms wide and nearly knocking Coleridge's drink from his hands. He swept his hands towards his own beer and drank deeply, much of it running down his front. Then he gasped, and grinned. 'The pain is gone!'

'Once again!' said his companion, and they clattered their pots together. 'It is the good stuff, is it not?'

Wilson ignored him again, sharing a momentary glance with two men who sat near the fire, hoping they wouldn't be brought into the conversation, because they'd heard it all before. The following moments were peaceful as the writers concentrated upon their drink – until Coleridge let out a small cry of distress, evidently because he'd finished. His eyes moved hopefully towards Wilson's. 'If it is your will, Will?' he said quietly.

'There is the matter of an account,' the innkeeper told him.

'It is not yet Friday!' the other protested.

'No. But you were to settle it last Friday.'

Coleridge stared at De Quincey, who shook his head sadly and finished his own drink. Then his expression brightened. 'A poem! You shall have a poem by way of payment!'

'No.' Wilson frowned. 'Never.'

'But this... this poem is of such quality! Such drama! Such...' he broke off, as if inspired, and shuffled in his pockets for a pencil and tablet, and spoke aloud as he scribbled: 'Lightly tripping o'er the fell; Deftly skimming o'er the... dale; Scarce our fairy wings bedew-ing... for the frothy mantling ale...'

'No,' Wilson repeated. 'Give me money or give me peace.'

'But, dear fellow!' De Quincey protested. 'Can you not see the magic waved before you? You have inspired the son of the greatest poet of our times! He writes for you! He writes *of* you!'

'And he did the same last month,' Wilson said. 'Same lines. Same day too, I think. Money, or peace.'

Coleridge looked up, looking hurt. 'Are you to scorn me, then?' he demanded. 'In this, my moment of creativity?'

'That's enough!' the innkeeper said, his voice every bit as men-acing as the sternest schoolteacher. 'Get out. And come back when you can pay.'

The pair made to complain, but Wilson raised himself on his heels and spread his arms outward, seeming to transform from a pleasant host to the worst kind of street villain. 'Out!' he bellowed.

Coleridge and De Quincey shot backwards, nearly falling into each other and the tables and chair behind them. Without another word they turned and threw themselves out through the door. There came a moment's muttering from outside, as they discussed where to go next – their shadows appeared against the uphill win-dow as they made to return to Ambleside; then against the downhill window as they decided their luck had run out, and to head home towards Grasmere.

'Babe so beautiful,' said one of the regulars, quoting a line Coleridge's father had written about his son.

THE AUCTION

Friday, November 6, 1835

NO ONE COULD BLAME JOHN HOLME if he'd taken too much of his own ale – because it wasn't going to be his for much longer.

The taproom was busier than usual for a Friday, but the crowd was split into two very distinct groups – the first, of regulars, who were there to support Holme in his misery; the second, of buyers, who hoped to profit from it.

'I reckon Barwise died at the right time,' said Tom, his nephew and innkeeper, offering John a fresh pot. 'Bad though it is to say.'

'You may be right,' John replied. 'And it's given me the chance to work with you these past five years. It's been appreciated. It won't be forgotten.' He didn't ask his innkeeper what the future held, because neither of them knew the answer. Instead, he went to hand over the coins he'd had in his hand for some time – but another regular, this time Old Sandy, pushed it away.

'This one's on me, John,' he said firmly. 'You're money's no good – there's a whole lot of us getting them in for you today.'

Holme nodded his thanks, unable to speak for the moment. His gaze was drawn to the figure of Rob Gray, near the fireplace, looking at the wall-clock. Gray turned away in time to lock eyes with Holme, and a look of shame flooded across his face. But Holme held up his pot and smiled. 'I hope you get it, lad,' he said. Rob had always liked the clock. His chance was about to come.

'Gentlemen!' cried an official-looking man, climbing the step from the sitting room in a black suit that made him appear almost like an funeral director. 'The auction will begin in ten minutes. Those interested will please take their places.'

One of the two groups in the room made to follow the official, including Rob and a handful of regulars who wanted to secure an item of personal value to them. Holme decided the proceedings could proceed without him.

He knew the regulars would be looking at him when he lifted the handbill to read it again, but it didn't matter. It was impossible to credit that seventy-nine years of ownership had resulted in the printing of a small piece of paper, that read: 'To be Sold by Auction: All that well-accustomed Inn, or Public House, known by the Sign of the Golden Rule, with the Brew-House, Barn, Stables and other Out-Buildings, thereto belonging and situated above the Stock in Ambleside.'

'You mustn't blame yourself,' Sandy said quietly, not for the first time. 'There's plenty of folk have come a cropper after the change of laws.'

Sandy was right. Only seven years ago the business had been doing better than many in the village wanted it to. The decrepit building had built a reputation among those travellers who valued friendly conversation and good beer above higher levels of physical comfort. And John Barwise had proved worthy of his name – a real asset when set against those who operated rival inns in the area.

But the changes had come fast. That same year a new law had made it possible for almost anyone to gain a license to brew ale – and even though most admitted the results were not the equal of the Rule's offerings, it seemed they weren't so far off as to dissuade some people from taking the cheaper options. A bolstered law two years later, which prevented those licensees from offering premises in which to drink it, was two years too late for many.

'The world's changing,' Holme said to no one in particular. 'Voting reform... the end of slavery... banning cock-fighting... the new road at the bottom of the hill, so folk don't even need to pass the door to go into the village. Maybe there's no use for this old place.'

'Away!' Sandy replied, gesturing towards the door. 'There's always need of a place to hide from that place out there.'

'Is there?' Holme said. 'Maybe you can't escape it. It's not fifty years since there were more jobs than people in Ambleside. Eighteen mills on the Stock, there were. Now look at us – extra taxation to help the poor, farmers struggling to make ends meet since the war ended, and Lord knows what else.'

Some of those in the taproom made to reply – but couldn't conjure up anything but desperately hopeful, and pointless, words. In the silence the preparations for the auction dominated everyone's thoughts. Rustling papers, low murmurs and businesslike coughs were the sounds to herald the end of a haven that had represented clattering pots, loud songs and wild jokes for more years than anyone within could tell of.

No one paid any heed to the door opening and closing, until the person who had entered offered his hand to Holme. 'John,' said the newcomer carefully.

'Tom Harrison!' Holme replied in surprise.

'Can I have a quick word?'

The pair disappeared into the brewery room above, while the regulars exchanged glances. 'Well, I never,' Sandy said. 'This might change everything.'

The quiet conversation didn't last long before the two men returned. Holme went back to his place near the barrels and raised his eyebrows in a signal to his nephew, while Harrison made his way towards the sitting-room.

'Tom!' Holme said loudly, causing the other to stop and turn round. 'Will you keep it open?'

The question was for the regulars, not for himself; and Harrison, the owner of the Church Stile Inn at Grasmere (which many had said was the twin of the Golden Rule), knew it.

'Aye,' he said equally loudly. 'Aye, I will that.'

THE COLD ROOM

Monday, September 16, 1839

GAYTHORNE PARKER LIKED THE RULE BEST when it was like this: him seated at the window, the sole customer, while Mary and Martha went about their work, and he took turns supporting them in their arguments in order to make sure they were always on the verge of argument. It meant he remained the focus of their conversation – or at least, he thought so.

'Now, Mary,' he said, 'You can't just dismiss it. There's years of evidence to suggest there's something to it.'

'There's years of idle gossip,' the older of the women replied. 'No evidence at all!'

'There's plenty, if you have to the eyes to see it,' young Martha told her. 'It's all around us, all the time.'

'Witchcraft! It's not so long since you'd get hung for even talking about it!'

'But it's not witchcraft, is it?' Gaythorne said. 'It's just the power of nature around us. The power of God, if you like.'

'And there's your reason for not talking about it in the pub,' Mary said. 'We'll leave it at that.'

'We'll leave it at that so you don't hear anything you don't like!' Gaythorne replied. 'Come on, Martha, make your point.'

'Well,' the servant began, 'where to begin? What about the lights in the sky these last few nights?'

'The aurora borealis,' Gaythorne nodded. 'Brighter than I've seen it in all my days.'

'So what?' Mary demanded.

'But there's much more than that,' Martha said. 'Them giant potatoes that grew in Kendal, when the rest of the crop died? The nut harvest bigger than it's ever been, but almost all of it's gone bad? What about that man who found the old Spanish coin, worth three pound, and died the same day?'

Mary shook her head. 'It's all just coincidence. I bet there's stranger things happening all over the place right now that you don't know about.'

'But that proves her point that something's going on,' Gaythorne argued. 'The more of it, the bigger whatever it is... is.'

'And what about the fox that chased the farmhand?' Martha asked.

'What about it?'

'Well, you can't say that's normal, can you? He goes out and shoots the fox dead, the hound goes up to collect it, and the thing gets up and chases them both into the woods.'

'Not your run-of-the-mill event, that,' Gaythorne agreed.

'Look,' Mary said, setting down her duster on the mantle. 'You can make a list as long as your arm of things that can't happen but did, that shouldn't happen but has, that won't happen but will. It doesn't prove anything, except we don't know everything about the world. So let that be an end to it!'

'But you haven't answered Martha's question,' Gaythorne said, an eyebrow raised, aware (and energised by the knowledge) that he was close to being shouted at. 'Did anything ever happen in that room?'

'No!' Mary shouted.

'*Something* did,' Martha replied, certainty on her young face. 'Either something did, or something's happened to someone who used to stay in the room. It were so cold last night.'

'It were so cold the aurora were out!' Mary replied. 'Weren't just that room.'

'But it wasn't the whole room,' the servant protested. 'Just by the fireplace. So cold it put my candle out.'

'Forget it. The last thing I need is some silly girl scaring herself out of her wits just because it were a bit on the cold side in her room.'

'I'm not scared. I'm just asking.'

Gaythorne had a thought. 'Ann Partridge used to stop in that room, years back,' he said. 'You won't remember her. She did your job, Martha, before she moved on. Beautiful girl, she was. But she sometimes used to sit at that fireplace, saying some right dark things.'

'You were in her room?' Mary cried. 'That's disgraceful!'

Gaythorne grinned. 'Ah, we were just young! We had an understanding for a time. Beautiful, she was. Might even have married her, if I were one for such things. But, aye, she used to sit there and talk about being destined for better things.'

'Every silly little girl says things like that,' Mary told him, glancing at Martha, who ignored the jab.

'It was the way she said it, though,' Gaythorne continued. 'Like she was angry it hadn't already happened. Like she deserved success, and she wanted to know why it wasn't already hers.'

'Nobody deserves success. If she wanted it, she'd have had to work for it.'

'I think she did,' the regular replied, staring into thin air as he remembered the old romance. 'Last I heard she'd got married and set up as a butcher with her man. Doing well too. But... I don't think that's what she meant, you know.'

'Silly girls and silly dreams,' Mary said dismissively.

'Nothing wrong in having ambitions,' Martha said strongly.

'You're right about that,' Gaythorne told her. 'I wonder where she is now... She was very beautiful.' Both women turned away from him as he stared into the middle-distance, until Leo Woodburn entered the taproom. 'Leo! Do you remember Ann Partridge?'

The newcomer shook his head sadly. 'You've heard, then. What a tragedy.'

'Heard what?'

Leo shook his head again, gesturing for Martha to pour him a drink, then taking two heavy draws before turning his eyes upward dramatically. 'Terrible, terrible, thing.'

'We haven't heard,' Gaythorne said. 'Tell us what's happened.'

'Ann. Sanderson, after she married.'

'Butcher's shop.'

'No, that failed. She went mad after it. Killed herself, just last night. Her and her five children. I just sorted the wood to make the coffins.'

Leo took another long drink. Martha gave Mary and Gaythorne a look that meant much more than anything she could have said.

JANE O'NEILL IN COURT AGAIN

Thursday, April 25, 1839

That Jane O'Neill was up in court again.

She pushes her luck, that one.

Selling brushes around the district without a license.

Well, she does, doesn't she?

She does indeed. And she keeps getting caught for it. But she does so well that she can afford to pay the fine, then she gets on with it until next time.

One day she'll get a fine she can't pay.

Not this time – magistrate let her off.

Let her off? Why? She'd done it, surely?

And she didn't deny it! But see, it were Peter Wells that took her to court. He weren't chasing her for the selling. He were chasing her for saying it were his brushes she were selling. He said it weren't his brushes.

Sounds like nonsense to me.

Well, he makes best brushes in Westmorland, he says.

I reckon he does, too. I use his.

So he says that, when Jane O'Neill tells folk they're buying his brushes, and they're not, she's doing his reputation a mischief.

Oh, right.

But the magistrate, he says that instead of doing him a mischief, she's doing him a favour by spreading his reputation! And it don't matter if she's selling his brushes or not, because the point is people want to buy his brushes, and that's good for his business, and so he shouldn't be chasing her at all!

Hold on...

So it got laughed out of court – and off goes Jane O'Neill, selling brushes that weren't made by Wells, until she gets caught next time!

I bought mine from her. Are you telling me they might not be Wells's brushes?

ROYAL VISIT

Tuesday, July 28, 1840

MATTHEW HARRISON LOVED HELPING OUT in the stables, so it was a special honour to be allowed to keep working there rather than elsewhere in the Golden Rule. The eight-year-old had been given responsibility for overseeing the regular trickle of visitors who came out of the pub's back door to peer at one particular horse.

'Is it a Barbary?' one asked as Matthew held up the lamp for their benefit.

'Might be an Arabian,' another said.

'It's summat special, you can tell that,' Matthew whispered.

It was a remarkable horse, all agreed, even if its rider appeared to be less so. A quiet, reserved, character, he sat near the fire with his supper, ignoring the level of interest his arrival an hour earlier had generated among the regulars.

'Well, he must be somebody,' slurred Stanley Greenwood, a labourer who lived in one of the cottages behind the pub.

'You leave him alone,' Matthew's father, Tom, said.

'I only want to ask how he came by the horse.'

'I'm warning you.' There had always been a certain doubt about Stanley's character – no one could prove anything (several had tried) but there remained the suspicion that, somewhere in England, he was wanted for a crime that shouldn't be discussed in front of gentlefolk. 'Make that your last tonight, Stanley.' Harrison felt it would be safer to minimise any risk.

'But...'

'You can talk to him in the morning if you're fit. He's staying at least two nights, he says.'

The innkeeper went about his work, and by the time he'd returned to the tables, Greenwood had gone, and so had the guest. Satisfied, he continued with his evening's work – unaware that things were not as straightforward as they seemed.

It was a trick Greenwood had used before. Inviting the guest to join him for a welcoming drink, he led him into the empty meeting room towards the back of the building, and had Mary Harrison serve him two pots of best beer through the hatch. Since Tom thought he'd gone, Tom wouldn't tell anyone to keep an eye out for him, and that meant he was free to ask anything he liked.

The problem was that Tom knew something about Greenwood that Greenwood appeared to keep forgetting about himself: and it was that, after a hard day's labouring, he tended to reach a point with his drinking such that one more mouthful was all it took to send him over a precipice.

So it was that, while Greenwood imagined a conversation that, perhaps, could wind up in the making of profit from a man with such a fine horse, the quiet guest found himself listening to a drunk regular talking about things he'd best have left unsaid.

'Are you with the dowager queen?' Greenwood asked. 'You probably are, God bless her. I hope she's enjoying what you might say is her retirement, since Queen Victoria took over, God bless her.

'She's staying at Low Nook with the Compstons, isn't she? Aye. Down the bottom of the hill there. A grand new road – I helped build it, I did. That and Compston Road and the new houses at Millans Park. I mean, some say it's been bad for business, now you can come and go through Ambleside without passing the Golden Rule. But you're here, aren't you? God bless you.'

The visitor said nothing, but nodded and shook his head when he felt it was appropriate, his expression betraying little more than a general sense of mild amusement.

'I should watch myself in case I commit what they call the 'loathsome and odious sin," Greenwood went on, referring to an ancient official description of drunkenness. 'But you're alright here. They look after you, send you home or up the stairs. You've come to the right place.

'Aye, God bless Queen Victoria. Oh, you should have been here for the coronation – although you were probably working, weren't you? Aye. It were a wonderful day, it were. Sun blazing down, free ale and port in Market Square. We had a triumphant arch outside here — oh, I'll tell you that story. You'll laugh at that!

'Well, with the new road open, see, the old one, Smithy Brow, out there, is no longer the only way into the village from this end. So when the magistrates raised a subscription for four arches, they took our money then said there'd be one on the North Road, at the Unicorn, one on Lake Road, at the other end, and a double-arch on Market Place. On account, said the magistrates, of its importance. And not on account, as we held, that they've always had it in for our Tom Harrison, for some reason.'

With another mouthful of beer, Greenwood's voice was notably wavering, and his pronunciation more difficult to follow. Yet he managed to rap the shelf on the serving hatch (having made sure Tom Harrison was not to be seen) and secure two more pots from Mary, before continuing.

'Well, we bloody made our own arch, didn't we! It were decided that, since we'd paid our fair share, it were not theft to take as what we needed from the makings of the other arches. It were easy if you're up at the time of the morning I am. No one else is, you see? So we made our own arch, quiet-like, and strike me if it weren't the best of the lot! It were in the papers if you don't believe me. Everyone noticed it.

'Aye, it were a great day. You'll know that Dr Hickie wrote new words for *God Save The Queen*? But our Hartley Coleridge, he wrote another set, and he got to do them twice – once in Market Place and once in the Salutation. There were a grand fire-balloon that went up at ten in the evening, when the dancing ended. And it landed near where it had been set off, so they set it off again! And the town band played, and the children marched, and... ah, it were a wonderful day for Queen Victoria, God bless her and her free drinks!

'So a few days later, the constable comes round here, and he's asking about our arch. Where did we get the parts, how did we do it without funding, you know the sort of thing. But we never telt him nowt – it's best to keep quiet, you know.

'Then the constable, he can't prove owt, but he says the Golden Rule sports day might be cancelled, on account of —' he struggled with the next phrase, attempting it several times — 'suspicions of felonious activity.

'Felonious! With most of the Ambleside Bond regular drinkers in here! So our Tom Harrison, he tells the constable that if the sports day is not to go ahead, then the constable had best take the half-pig donated as a prize by Lord Burghersh, and tell Lord Burghersh why Ambleside don't want it.

'Well, that shut the constable up! Off he goes, on his way. All we had to do after that was find ourselves a half-pig, and tell people it were donated by Lord Burghersh. I mean, he'll never know – he's probably not heard of the Golden Rule, never mind the sports day.

'So that were easy. We got a half-pig, we had the sports day, we got away with the arch, and eighteen-thirty-eight were a grand summer! But I need to tell you —'

'Stanley Greenwood!' snarled Tom Harrison from the meeting-room door. 'You get out of here this minute.' The labourer went to protest. 'Now!' Harrison bellowed, and the word sent him on his way (as well as silencing the taproom).

Harrison turned to the visitor, unsure of how to proceed. 'Sorry about that,' he said calmly, his years as an innkeeper informing his act of nothing being wrong. 'He's a bit of a local character. Just makes things up.'

'Oh, it's perfectly alright,' the guest replied, with his accent from far away that was slightly difficult to follow. 'I didn't understand a word!'

A FINAL WARNING

Monday, April 13, 1846

MIKE AITCHISON, Harry Barrow, Ronald Bell, Victor Coupe and Frank Dodd sipped their ale in silence, which wasn't like them. Normally the fuss around their table was such that staff barely escaped with their lives while serving fresh drinks or recovering empty pots.

Aitchison and Barrow could start a conversation on arrival that continued – with countless interruptions – until they were incoherent with drink, but still apparently able to understand each other. Coupe and Dodd seemed to instinctively know which side the other would take on any given news item of the day, and automatically take the other side, then spend the evening trying to force others to agree. and the well-named Bell would often have to be coerced into not singing with the promise of a free top-up, which only worked until he thought of another song.

But not this day. Instead, the five men sat around their usual table in the centre of the taproom, saying absolutely nothing.

William Black entered his pub via the back door, threw his hat and cane into a corner and loosened the uncomfortable collar of his best suit. He glared at the regulars, who hid behind their pots while staring back at him, white-eyed. He grabbed himself a pot and poured himself a full pint of the best – usually he only took a third of mild. He drank more than half of it, his back to the room, before turning round.

'Got away with it,' he said, staring at his friends one at a time.

'What, entirely?' Bell asked after a pause.

'Aye.'

'Not even a fine?'

'Not even a fine.' He'd been facing a fifty-pound levy for his offence, and even the risk of losing his victualler's license.

'So... we're all right, then?'

'All right!' Black shouted, and the stress of the day pushed through him with full force. 'All right! That's the third time I've been up for opening during Divine Service of a Sunday. The third time! God knows how they didn't throw the book at me. I might even have been ruined!'

He calmed as quickly as he'd exploded. 'It's a stupid law,' he complained. 'Happen I'm not the only one to have broken it these last seven years. Happen I'm not the worst for it, either. Rob Akew was up with me for the same thing at the Royal Oak. They let him off too. Bound over for two months, so if we do it again, they'll come down hard.' He sighed. 'So, aye, all right. But still, things have got to change.'

The regulars looked down. It wasn't essential to be drinking on a Sunday morning – but it felt good to be cheating the magistrates, pushing back against those who seemed determined to make life harder than it was. They'd have to find another way to express that need.

'Aye, things have got to change,' Black said quietly, then held his hands out towards his companions. 'So, for the love of God, when I open for you on Sunday morning in June, *keep the bloody noise down!*'

BONA FIDE TRAVELLING

Sunday, September 10, 1854

'MA, HOW COME the people who drink here on Sunday is different from them as drink here the rest of the week?'

Ann Black was proud of young Geordie's question – he was learning fast. And he had need of it, since her husband and his father's death the previous year. He'd become the man of the house, and very quickly realised that collecting pots, tending the fire and cleaning the lamps were suddenly the least of his worries.

'It's another stupid new law,' she told him. She was aware that he'd noticed her change in attitude towards him – no more treating him as a young lad, the apple of her eye, but instead unveiling the harsh realities of life – but that was how it had to be.

'There's a lot of folk, rich folk, who seem to have nothing better to do but tell the rest of us how to life,' Ann went on. 'The folk who come in here want to get out of their troubles, and they want to have a nice drink with their friends. But these rich folk think they don't deserve it, and they want to stop it.

'The latest trick is to tell folk they're not allowed to be in a pub on a Sunday. The only exception is what they call "bona fide travellers" – that's folk who aren't locals and can prove it.'

'So our regulars can't drink here on a Sunday,' Geordie said, before waving across the taproom. 'And these folk, they're regulars from somewhere else, as "bona fide travellers" – while our regulars are somewhere else as "bona fide travellers!"'

She smiled. 'Good lad!' She said, 'But think on – there's always another stupid law if you wait long enough. They banned cock-fighting indoors so it's done outdoors now. They banned labourers from waiting in pubs for work, so they stand out the back while they wait. They banned folk from collecting their wages from pubs, so they do that elsewhere now as well. They won't be happy till no one is allowed in here.'

Ann put her arm on his shoulder. He'd soon be taller than her, and he was going to be a good-looking man. 'That's why pubs are so important, Geordie,' she told him. 'Our folk work their fingers to the bone while rich folk sit in big houses and work out how to make lives worse. In here, they get to escape from that for a while.

'And you ignore that temperance lot as well. Anyone as says a pub is all about drinking doesn't know what they're talking about. It's about people, Geordie. Pubs are about people. Never forget that.'

It was the advice she'd heard her husband giving staff time and time again until his death. She hoped it would live on, since he hadn't been able to.

FROM SAD SHIRES

Sunday, July 19, 1857

PRIVATE JACK MARTIN could no longer tell if it was late evening, or if his sight was fading. He knew both were coming. He lay on his back, wondering if the man nearby who was breathing far too quickly and loudly might stop soon. Then he realised it was him, and tried to control himself.

Bithoor. An alien town in an alien country. What had he been thinking of, joining up and following General Havelock to India? It had seemed like a bright future. And even though he'd been told the British had won, it seemed there was neither brightness, nor a future.

He imagined it would be a fine old evening in the Golden Rule. Meg would be giggling as she served beers. Malcolm would be sitting in the corner making jokes no one could hear. Wilf and Nora would be having one of those arguments that went nowhere and meant nothing. Rob and Jim would be planning their next point-less, but hilarious, adventure. Donald Hodge would be hoping for the chance of a cuddle from Margaret. Well, he might get it too.

Oh, but it was so dark now. So dark he could see the rafters above the taproom, their horse brasses twlnkling over the candles. He could hear the massed tones of murmured conversations from the sitting room and the meeting room, beyond the general noise of the main area where people spoke, laughed and sang at a joyous cacophony of different volumes.

A pint. Just the one, then top the pot up with thirds. That's the way to drink, Meg – that's the way the old men do it, and we should learn from them. Listen and learn. What are they saying? Another pint? No, but a top-up. Another third. Then another.

I remember you wrote to me about the new town hall they're building at Market Place. It sounds lovely – new shops too, for us to stand outside while you make lists of what you'll buy when we're married. Why don't we go and take a look? Right now? Let's sneak out. No one notices when we sneak out for a little kiss; or if they do, they let us away with it.

No. No, you're right, Meg. Let's just stay here, stand against the fire in the taproom, and have another top-up. Let's not leave. Let's never leave the Rule. Let's buy it, let's run it, let's welcome everyone for ever and let's never leave. I don't want to leave, because I'm only twenty-one and I haven't married you yet and I'm dying and

It had been a strangely subdued night in the pub. Meg Black locked the front door, turned down the fire then snuffed out the candles. She felt very, very sad, but she didn't know why.

THREE YEARS' BAD LUCK

Wednesday, March 16, 1859

It's your good self!

I saw it were open – I had to come in.

Aye, it's open. Staying open.

What happened?

Well, that's John Cowell away. I don't know how many folk, if any, bid for the let, but in the end Matthew's taken it.

Matthew?

Who better? He's worked here man and boy, and his dad's still the owner. And the Rule came into their family by an auction an'all.

The more things change they more they stay the same. Poor John, though.

Ah, he were never right for this place. He were too friendly, like.

Nowt wrong with that, surely?

If you ask me, an innkeeper's got to keep his distance, up to a point. There's rules. It's his house, see, and we pay to be in it, and as long as no one has to say that it's all well and good. But you're only going to be so close to a man as you pay for your entertainment. It's friendly, aye, but it's still business.

I had a lot of time for John Cowell.

Some did, some didn't. Don't matter now, does it?

I still think it were the gambling. He weren't much of a drinker, but I think he were a big one for the cards and all that.

I've nowt against playing games. But if you ask me, a tanner's enough for any working man to lose in a game. If you're going over that, you're getting it wrong.

Poor John. Of course, that's the second time in three years he's lost everything, in't it?

Oh aye, I were forgetting.

Poor bugger sold his shop to buy the lease of this place. Night before he moves in, the shop burns down, with all his property in it. No insurance.

And his savings. He should have that in a bank. If you ask me, any man has more than a week's wages in cash on him is asking for trouble.

He always said he were cursed.

I don't hold with that nonsense.

Still, though – look at him. Sold the shop, lost everything. Worked hard in here, maybe didn't quite get it right, lost everything again.

It weren't for the want of folk helping him, neither.

That's right! Folk making a point of coming in here instead of going somewhere else, just to make him a few bob to keep him going. He never knew, of course, did he?

Doubt it. Too busy gambling or cozying up too close to people.

Still, when you look at it like that, though, adding in what he didn't know, you can see why it could be said he were cursed.

Might be right.

LIFELONG STUDY

Saturday, April 27, 1861

Dear Sirs —

You reported in your pages that the Dean of Carlisle gave a speech on the subject of temperance, writing: 'He had ascertained when he was at Ambleside, that the number of deaths among publicans in that small village was fearful. In fact there was but one man among them that had lived in that occupation for any length of time. No climate was so deadly as the occupation of a publican. No man could sell those poisons without a curse upon him, and that curse was a short life.'

*Might I suggest that, if the Dean of Carlisle's aim on this
Earth is to preserve life, that he might avoid vexing that of
Ambleside's publicans with the dissemination of such utter tosh?*

Yours faithfully

*Thomas Harrison, owner, The Golden Rule Inn
(Aged 76)*

OLD DAN'S LAST BREW

Monday, September 25, 1865

MATTHEW FOLDED THE LETTER and wrapped an envelope
around it, then sealed it with wax, scribbled an address on the front
and put it in his pocket. He'd usually take young James with him
to the post office, but he wanted to go alone. A man of his position
in the world usually enjoyed the short walk along North Road,
but not today – today he offered well-wishers a grim smile; and
fortunately, all those who knew him took the hint.

He said nothing in the post office and nothing on the way back
along the road. Entering the Rule by the yard-gate, passing the
stables, cottages and all the paraphernalia of brewing, he took a
deep breath before stepping through the back door. Everything was
going to be different after the next conversation.

The doorway took him straight into the brewery, where Dan Gill
was working away as fast as he always had. A sprightly figure that
confounded his years, there was no doubting that he was happy in
his tasks, and always had been, and would always have been – given
the chance.

'Dan...' Matthew said slowly.

'Yes, Mr Harrison,' the brewer smiled.

'I have to talk to you.'

'I know,' he said. 'Been a long time coming. But I knew it were.'

'Things have changed, Dan. Nothing stays the same.'

'Nor does it.' The old man continued about his work among the fireplace, the water vats, the mixing cauldrons, the pipes, cups and barrels. 'No matter whether we want it to or not.'

'Times are difficult,' the innkeeper went on. 'If it wasn't for the farm we'd have had to sell years ago.'

'I know that too,' Dan replied flatly.

'I've made an arrangement,' Matthew said, drawing a breath to say the rest in one go, 'to have beer bought in from an outside brewer. I need the space to bring in more customers.'

'Won't be the same,' Dan said, betraying nothing.

'No. No, it won't. Nothing to match the beer you've made here, Dan. Nothing ever will.'

'Wouldn't have thought so. No call for good beer in the coming years – just for lots of cheap beer.'

'I think I've done alright... considering,' Matthew replied.

'What will you do with the space?'

'Well, this lower area is to become another sitting room. There's to be a floor laid above, so it's the same height as the taproom, and there's to be a ballroom along from the bedrooms upstairs.'

Dan nodded, but didn't look towards Matthew. 'Makes sense, I suppose. More seats for bums below, more space for feet above. You'll near double your capacity.'

'Aye,' the innkeeper sighed. 'And there's a beer engine coming, with hand pumps along a bartop for the taproom. And a cellar that'll need looking after. So there's still work for you here, Dan, if you want it.'

'And what else would I do, at sixty-seven year old? Of course I'll stop here.' He finally looked at Matthew. 'Will you let me do one thing?'

'One more October brew?'

'Best of the year, every year,' he said. 'Bed it down and it'll be good until I'm gone.'

'It's even in the contract with the brewer,' Matthew smiled. 'And a small consideration for you on top.'

Dan smiled. In truth he'd expected the news every year for the past decade, and it was probably the only thing in his life that had given him serious cause for concern. Now it was happening, it didn't seem as bad as he'd always feared it would. Mr Harrison was no bad master, and he'd done the best he could to hold off the inevitable. In the end it was always going to come to this.

The old man lifted two pots and went over to a small cask that only he was allowed to go near. He tapped it, filled the pots and handed one to Matthew. 'This here room's been a brewery for three hundred and eleven years, as best as I can reckon it.'

'I think you're about right.'

'Well, here's to all three hundred and eleven of them,' Dan said, clattering his pot against Matthew's.

The innkeeper made a noise of satisfaction – partly for the taste, and partly because the difficult conversation had ended. 'Tell you what, Dan, they'll never brew anything like this.'

'No, they won't,' the old man replied. They drank in silence, looking round the old room, both struggling to imagine how it might be laid out in a year's time, before Matthew handed back his empty pot, nodded, and went through into the taproom.

THE TURNPIKE SAILOR

Thursday, March 5, 1868

1.00PM: Jane Harrison was a happily-married woman, and she'd heard all the best (and worst) approaches imaginable from a wide range of menfolk in the taproom – yet even she struggled to take her eyes off the cheery character who'd just bidden her good-day.

'It's a wet winter, it is, but at least it's not like the snow we had last year. Could you believe that?' he asked, his dimpled cheeks ready to burst into a wider smile than the one he already wore, his dark eyes smiling too, his strong chin and generous build offering every welcome a girl might want on a cold day.

'But will I let it bother me? I will not! Because I'm home from sea after a long, successful voyage – and I have fifty pound to be spent before I go back!' He sat down by the fire and opened his slightly worn coat to reveal an even more worn suit of clothes beneath. He looked into the air, making a performance of a decision to be made, then looked Jane straight in the eye with a disarming, almost embarrassing admiration. 'Best steak,' he grinned. 'With everything alongside. And I mean the best. And best ale too. Will you join me? Say you will – I'm celebrating!'

Jane was even more embarrassed by how long it took her to reply; it seemed like minutes before she muttered a shy welcome to the Golden Rule, poured a pot of the best and called on Sarah to start work in the kitchen.

'You've only ordered one!' the visitor said sadly.

'I have my work to do,' she replied, immediately regretting that she sounded angry (she didn't feel it).

His face fell – but only for a moment. 'Maybe later, then,' he said with a new smile. 'I like it here. I think I'll spend a good bit of that fifty pound in here. You'll have tea with me one day... and maybe something more!' He allowed the suggestion to hang in the air long enough for her to begin reacting, before adding: 'Coffee, wine, sherry – whatever it is, you'll have it on me, with my thanks for such a wonderful, friendly welcome! Robert Roskell,' he continued, holding out his hand. 'Call me Rob.'

Jane was becoming angry at last, but at herself, for not being able to deal with one charming, good-looking customer after all her years of owning an inn alongside her husband. She got closer to anger still when she held out her hand to be shaken, and instead had it taken by the palm and kissed, while Roskell stared into her eyes, making all manner of suggestions with his own.

'I'll go and see about your steak,' she said quickly, turning away. He watched her go, his gaze intent, before he smiled again and turned his concentration onto his ale.

1.45PM: Roskell looked like the perfect man in repose, his third pot of best before him, a large cigar in his hand, his legs stretched towards the fire and his head to the heavens. He'd just finished telling a story of one of his adventures at sea, on a voyage that had been planned to last eighteen months but continued for four years in the end – hence his handsome reward at its end.

'So it was all worth it, and now I have three months, maybe more, of doing nothing before I head off again.' He sat upright and turned to Jane. 'You keep steaks like those coming, and beer like that too, and I won't be going anywhere else. Although —' his tone changed — 'I think I'd better get myself some rooms. I'd rather have a bit of space, since I'm going to be here for a while. And I don't think I trust myself to stay under your roof!'

Jane, who'd recovered her poise, just smiled back with one raised eyebrow. 'Well, there are a few places I can recommend,' she said.

'What would the nearest be? You know, for convenience.'

'Beth Barrow has rooms to let,' she told him. 'Just round the corner on Mill Row. 'I'm sure they'd do you fine.'

'Is she on her own there?' he asked.

'No, her husband's there too.'

'That's good,' he said. 'Saves any suggestion of... impropriety. Talking of which, would you write me a note of introduction? I'll take that round and get it sorted right now. Then I can come back here.'

It didn't take long to write a brief letter, by which time Roskell was ready for the short journey. 'But first, I have a small favour to ask,' he said, leaning in conspiratorially. 'Would you keep something for me? For safety. I don't want to be carrying it around with me all day – you never know who's around you.' He pulled out a thick envelope, and waved it in a manner that suggested its contents were relatively light.

'There's a strongbox in the back,' Jane said.

'Yes, that would be sensible,' he replied, nodding slowly, without taking his eyes away from hers.

She led him behind the bar into the kitchen behind the taproom, and took the envelope from him after he'd made certain to demonstrate it was sealed. There could be little doubt that it was full of banknotes. 'That's not all of it,' Roskell said quietly. 'The rest is with my luggage, on the way from Barrow. I thought it was sensible to split it up, you know.'

'There's been a few footpads around in the last couple of weeks,' she said, agreeing. 'It makes sense to be careful.'

He mouthed 'thank you' and turned to leave, before setting eyes on young Sarah. 'Ah, the mistress of the kitchen!' he cried, taking her by both hands and receiving an excited whoop in response. 'And a fine cook you are too! I'll be having more from you – supper for a start!' He flashed a grin at the servant before flashing another one at Jane. 'Back soon,' he said, and strode off.

Jane went to write up Roskell's account before she forgot about it. She was mildly irritated at his reaction to meeting Sarah – a nice girl, to be sure, but terribly plain.

3.20PM: 'You don't have a sister, do you? I'm so sorry! That was terribly inappropriate!' Roskell made a face like a naughty school-boy, and Jane wasn't surprised to discover it only added to his charm.

He'd returned around half an hour earlier, professing himself delighted with Beth Barrow's rooms and rate, noting that, at twenty-five shillings a week, it left him plenty to spend in the Rule. And to that end, he'd enquired if it might be acceptable to settle at the end of the day, when his luggage had arrived via the White Lion, so he could account for all his money at the same time.

In the meantime he'd enjoyed a heavy pork lunch and two more pots of best beer, and told a story about how his ship had come close to running out of drinking-water while lost on an alien sea. 'Your man Coleridge had it right,' he said, before expressing sadness at learning that Samuel Taylor's son, Hartley, had died seventeen years previously – he hadn't known, but had known that the young poet was known to frequent the Rule, and he'd harboured hopes of a meeting. 'To absent friends, even if we never met!' he grinned, raising his pot – and Jane felt certain she could detect a bitter sadness behind his words.

'But I am thinking of settling down. Getting married, and everything,' he went on, his glance caught briefly by Sarah in the background. 'How long have you been married, Jane?'

'Twelve years,' she said, making a point of speaking strongly. 'Very happily.'

'Good! That's good!' Roskell replied, raising his pot once more. 'Seventeen years late for Coleridge, twelve years late for — anyway, I won't get far with a good woman in these clothes, will I? Come on, be honest.'

Jane paused for a moment before admitting that his outfit was in need of some careful attention. 'Parker and Head are very good,' she offered. 'On the New Road, not far along from your rooms.'

'There's still time – and I really should check on my luggage,' Roskell said. 'Jane, your note to Beth Barrow was perfect. A man my size must be careful not to seem imposing. Do you think you could write me a note for Mr Parker and Mr Head?'

She was happy to oblige, her thoughts full of how village trade at its best could see everyone benefitting from the visit of someone who was extended a warm welcome. The note written, another kiss to the hand received, and assurance given that his envelope of banknotes remained safe in the strongbox, Roskell set off, with the stated aim of returning within the hour, dressed in the latest fashion, with the intent of sweeping Jane off her feet.

5.00pm: 'A pint, John?' Jane asked as Constable Craigie entered the pub.

'No, Jane – a word, if you have a moment,' he replied, nodding to all present and gesturing with his head that they should speak elsewhere.

'Did you write a couple of notes for one Robert Roskell today?' the policeman asked once they were in the empty kitchen.

'Yes, I did,' she said. 'Is something wrong? Is he alright?'

He swayed his head and put on an awkward expression. 'Well, it seems there's more to him than meets the eye,' he said at last. 'He had himself a steak at Beth Barrow's place, and went off with a bundle of linen to make fresh underclothes, then he got himself a new outfit at Parker and Head, and left his old clothes there for repair.'

Jane nodded. 'That's what he said he'd do.' But she knew there was something amiss.

'Well,' said the constable, 'He said he'd collect his clothes, and settle his bill, within the hour, and he didn't come back. He'd spoken about collecting his luggage at the White Lion —'

'He said that to me, too.'

'— Only he's never been heard of there. Nor the Salutation, nor the post office, and there's nowhere else the luggage could be delivered to, except here.'

Jane shook her head. 'It wasn't.'

'Then... a man fitting his description, with brand-new clothes, was seen on the mail coach south, just after four,' Craigie continued. 'I have to ask you, Jane – does he owe you anything?'

She sighed. 'A confidence man?'

'They call it the 'turnpike sailor' routine,' he replied. 'He comes in with a story of shore leave with unpaid wages, only he's waiting for the money to arrive, then takes what he can get before moving on. The only sailing he does is between inns on the turnpike roads.'

'Oh, no...' She'd probably known it all along – the experience of her years had been flashing a warning from the back of her mind all day. Roskell had been good, but she should have been better. Then she remembered he'd spoken of the heavy snows last winter. Why would he mention that if he'd been at sea for four years?

Jane went to the strongbox and recovered the envelope. 'He gave me this for safe-keeping,' she told Craigie, handing it over. She wasn't surprised when the constable tore it open to reveal folded sheets of blank paper.

Matthew Harrison came back from a long, hard shift on the wet farmlands. 'What a day I've had!' he cried, tired but happy with his efforts. 'Afternoon, John – will you have a drink?'

'Matt...' Jane began.

STILL AND SILENCED

Friday, May 23, 1873

TOM HARRISON WOULD ALWAYS ALLOW that one never stopped learning from the day of birth until that of death – and indeed considered it entirely possible that learning continued afterwards. But in his many years of innkeeping he hadn't experienced the turn of events explained to him by his son.

'I can't understand,' said Matthew, staring at the bottle store as if it might answer. 'All of a sudden, about six months ago, people just stopped buying spirits. Almost entirely. We sold nearly none for six months.

'Then, just as suddenly, earlier this week people are buying again – similar to the amounts we sold before.'

Tom had spent all day considering the situation, and it had distracted him from his usual enjoyment of the newspaper.

Then things changed as suddenly as they appeared to have done twice before. Rising from his seat, Tom grabbed the newspaper between both hands and read aloud to the busy taproom.

'A revenue officer of Kendal has discovered a most ingenious cave between Ambleside and Coniston,' he said, 'fitted up for illicit distillation.

'It was excavated in a precipitous bank, far away from the public road, the roof supported by flags and posts. Rain was kept out, but a stream of water could be turned into the cave whenever required.

'There was a complete apparatus and materials for distillation. No one was found in the cave.'

He folded the newspaper as loudly as he could and slammed it on the mantle as he walked out. Only his son saw the glimmer of mirth in his eyes – and struggled not to share it as he finally understood the meaning of his regulars' recent downcast expressions.

A BAD THROW

Wednesday, July 15, 1885

That fellow was up in court for breaking that window up the road the other night.

Oh aye?

Aye. Said he were staying here and couldn't get in late at night, and he were only trying to wake someone by throwing stones up.

Seems fair enough.

Gave his occupation as ventriloquist.

Can't be a very good one, eh? If he can't throw his voice instead of a stone.

That's what I thought...

FENCED OFF

Saturday, October 19, 1878

Dear Sirs —

Mr. Makereth claimed in The Westmorland Gazette last week that the Footpaths Committee and I showed 'nothing but contempt for me and my land' when we broke down his fence and took a stroll to Stock Ghyll Force.

My feelings, and those of the committee, on Mr. Makereth's fence-building, and the charging of threepence per entrant to visit the waterfalls, is well known. I should like to think that my history of taking strong and decisive action in the field of battle, whether home or abroad, is also well known.

I shall not comment on the upcoming legal action,
but I should like to correct Mr. Makereth's statement.
We did not show 'nothing but contempt' — on the contrary,
we offered him tea when he confronted us.

There might have been a glass of wine, or, dare I suggest it,
a pint of ale, had he not taken such violent offence to being
invited to the Golden Rule Inn with us.

Yours etc —

Lt. Col. Rhodes

CALLING IN THE TABS

Wednesday, March 23, 1887

Bill Copley's calling in all the tabs.

Again?

He's furious about the railway not coming. As if that's our fault.

It were never coming, not as soon as Wordsworth wrote that poem back in, what were it, forty-four?

Well, they've been a long time deciding it.

No they haven't. They've been a long time looking *as if they were deciding it. I told Bill that many a time. He took on this place twelve, thirteen year ago, thinking the railway were coming, and counting money he'd never earned. He were always a tight-fisted get.*

Remember he sued Harriet Townson? Saying she'd forced one of his cows over a garden wall and killed it?

That cow fell. Everyone knew it.

Then he were angry when he lost the case, and had to pay costs. He called in all the tabs that time an'all.

Aye... I always said it made no difference to me whether the railway came or not. But there were one thing I read that made me think. Someone said as how people who wanted to enjoy the scenery would be better getting off train at Windermere and coming along road to Ambleside. It's only five mile. That way, he says, they're not just looking at scenery out window – they're in it.

Bill's not interested in all that. He don't want them on the road, or anywhere else, when they should be in here giving him their money, he reckons.

Reckon he'll put prices up?

He can try...

You'll pay it. You always do. Where else do you want to drink?

I know that. Problem is, so does Bill.

OFFICIAL CONCERN
Friday, August 25, 1899

Dear Sirs —

We thank the large number of citizens of Ambleside and Liverpool who have made enquiries about the condition of Mr William Oulton, Lord Mayor of Liverpool, after his unfortunate accident in Ambleside on Wednesday.

They will be glad to learn that Mr Oulton is in good spirits following the incident, and it is expected that he will make a full recovery from the shock and bruises within a few days.

We should like your readers to be aware that certain ill rumours regarding the accident are completely unfounded and outrageous.

Mr Oulton was simply resting against the wall of the Golden Rule Hotel when he lost his footing. We utterly repute the suggestion that the Chief Magistrate of one of Britain's greatest cities had spent some time within, teaching a certain song to other patrons.
The claim is disgraceful and unthinkable.

Mr Oulton denies even knowing the song, particularly the disgusting third verse. We trust this brings the matter to a close.

Yours etc —

Mr S Winnings, the Office of the Lord Mayor of Liverpool

LOCATING THE LAKE
Friday, July 4, 1902

So, it turns out Windermere is in Lancashire, not Westmorland.

What's this nonsense?

Says so here, in paper. There was a fellow up on court for fishing without a license on Windermere, and he were charged with committing the offence in the county of Lancashire.

I always thought Windermere were in Westmorland.

So did he – his solicitor asked for the charge to be changed, but the magistrate went on with it and fined him ten shillings, as being committed in Lancashire.

Haven't they been fighting about that for months, whether Windermere's in Westmorland or Lancashire?

Aye.

Amazing, isn't it? All that wisdom and learning, and magistrates and judges and lawyers don't know where the biggest lake in England is. I'll tell 'em – 'It's just down the road, there!' No charge.

FETCH THE SHOTGUN

Saturday, November 19, 1904

THE THICK SNOW that lay over the village absorbed many of the usual sounds around Smith Brow – but not this one. With a muffled regular thud and the uniform voices, many of them pitched higher than they could properly achieve, there was no doubting that the Salvation Army had arrived.

'Oh, bloody hell, no,' said Bertie Thomas, leaning as he always did near the bar hatch. 'You'd best stop them coming in, lad.'

Jimmy Walker was struggling with the amount of people demanding served, never mind dealing with anything else, as the door flew open and a dozen uniformed singers marched in.

It was a typical Ambleside lights weekend – the tradition of the third Saturday in November, when Christmas celebrations began with a procession through the town, a seasonal fair, and extra drinking all round. That, of course, brought out the Salvation Army in force, especially since the temperance argument had become a hot one in recent years. Every innkeeper had, through time, devised their own methods for dealing with the onslaught of pamphleteers and lecturers, who aimed to disrupt the evening's proceedings in his hostelry. If they couldn't persuade anyone to forsake the demon drink for ever, then perhaps they could coerce them into abandoning it for the evening, by making the experience of being in the pub a less pleasant one than usual.

Joseph Jackson had been a master of the game. But Joseph

Jackson had recently died, leaving his pub without a master, his regulars without guidance, and young Jimmy completely out of his depth.

'They're inside now,' Bertie warned the barman, raising his pot to his mouth to hide his smile. 'Jackson would never have let them get them that far.'

'You're right about that, God rest his soul,' said Norman Garside from his usual place at the other end of the bar. 'Jackson would have had his shotgun out by now.'

'Shotgun?' the young server cried, panic in his voice, as he tried to pump pints, serve them, take payment and set up fresh pots all in a single move. Meanwhile, the soldiers of the Lord had spread out among the busy throng, delivering leaflets and asking for contributions in return.

'Aye, it'll be in the back,' Bertie said. 'I'll fetch it if you want.'

'See as it's loaded,' Norman advised. 'Jackson always set off a round or two.'

'You can't do that!' Jimmy said desperately.

'Well, you must do something,' Bertie told him.

'Tell them to gerrout!' Norman said. 'Before they start bloody singing!'

'Singing?' Jimmy repeated, shocked. 'Everyone will leave!'

'Everyone is,' Bertie said, gesturing with his head towards the handful of people who were making for the door.

Jimmy tried to look in every direction at once, while continuing the rough ballet performance of pouring, serving and charging. The result was inevitable – one of the pots he held crashed to the floor, causing him to lose his balance, and soon he joined it along with several other pots for good measure.

The clattering brought a temporary silence to the room, into which Bertie, his hand over his mouth for misdirection, shouted:

'Give us a song!'

The Salvation Army didn't need asking twice. They burst into a rough performance of *All People That On Earth Do Dwell* – and within seconds they were joined by the louder, and less controlled, voices of the regulars, who kept missing the end of each line for their laughter.

'You're in trouble now, lad,' Bertie said with the face of a schoolmaster, as young Jimmy sat, bewildered, in a mess of broken pots, beer and embarrassment.

A MAN NEEDS HIS PUB

Thursday, September 20, 1906

Has Harry Salkeld been in?

Never! You won't see him in here again. He ran off without paying his tab, didn't he? Charlie Wearing's barred him.

I think you *will* see him in again. I saw him the other day – and he were talking to Charlie Wearing.

What, without fists being thrown?

Aye. It were quite funny... I saw him coming up Church Street, but he didn't see me. Who did see him was the vicar – and he went racing straight into Harry's face! Tore strips off him for not being in church, told him he'd have his name read out, or fined, or worse, if he weren't in his pew on Sunday.

Bloody 'ell. That's last thing old Harry needs, with his problems, poor bugger. He's having a hard time, no doubt.

He is that – he's barred from everywhere else an'all. So Harry goes on his way, and he still doesn't see me, then who does he run into on Lake Road but Charlie Wearing!

What a day!

That's what I thought. But I wanders past, just to see what's what, you know. And Charlie's saying to him, 'Look, I know times are hard, Harry, and I know you can't pay off your tab. But at times like this a man needs his pub – so you come back in, buy your drinks and don't ask for no credit, and I'll wipe the tab.'

Charlie Wearing said that?

Aye, he did, and I heard him first-hand. So you'll be seeing Harry Salkeld in again, I reckon. A man that's having his life and times could do with a drink.

Good old Charlie...

IN PLAIN SIGHT

Wednesday, February 7, 1912

I'm not bloody having it, I tell you. It's a liberty beyond all liberties.

What are you on about now?

The windows.

What about them?

They're talking about a new law, that pub windows have to be clean and see-through, and no curtains while it's open.

Bloody liberty! Why?

They think folk will stop drinking if they can be seen.

Oh...

How's a man to enjoy a quiet pint away from the world when the whole bloody world's looking in and watching him?

More of this temperance rubbish.

I tell you, if that happens I'll have to move pubs.

Why don't you start drinking in the back sitting room? The windows only look onto the yard there.

If I'm drinking away from the taps I might as well be in another pub. Go into the back room? I'm not a bloody woman.

No, you're not...

And there's another thing. I'm not having my bloody wife able to look in the window and know I'm here!

But she always knows you're here. Because you're always here!

Aye... well...

A GOOD PLAN

Saturday, September 14, 1915

Did you hear what's happening in Carlisle?

About the pubs?

Aye. Government taking them all over to control the market.

The main reason, I hear, is to keep a lid on how much the folk at the armaments factories drink.

There is a war on, after all.

Aye. You can see the point, can't you? What were that fella over at Elterwater, back in eighty-five, eighty-six? Mawson?

Mawson – that's him. Went to work on the gunpowder mix, full of drink, fell in the saltpetre mix and got scalded to death.

Some say he were in charge the year before, when the whole place blew up. He were drunk then an'all.

So you can see their point. I hear there's to be a law against buying rounds – you're only allowed to buy for yourself.

I can think of plenty of folk who'd be happy with that.

Oh, aye.

They're bringing it in at a few places in Scotland, too. Private landlords to sell up, government coming in, making sure drink doesn't interfere with the war effort.

It makes sense.

It makes a lot of sense.

Better not happen here, though.

Better not.

RETURNING HERO
Friday, June 30, 1916

THE SUN SMILED DOWN in welcome to an enthusiastic crowd, who'd gathered to extend their own welcome to one of their own: a hero, decorated just recently for his bravery on the front, and discharged with great honour.

'He were such a handsome lad,' said one woman, with a wink.

'That he were,' said her companion. 'Oh, and that smile!'

'Leave him be!' a man shouted. 'He's a man now, and a good one too. And anyhow, you lot are too old for him. He's still, what, twenty two, twenty three year?'

'He'll want to learn a thing or two...' grinned the first woman.

But amid the waving flags, the Windermere brass band playing the *Rushbearing Song* that they'd learned specially (the ceremony was taking place the following day), and the general spirit of release, a gloom grew up from a space that appeared around the procession that made its way up the hill.

'I can't see him!' said an onlooker. 'You'd think he'd stand on back of car.'

Then it became clear that he couldn't. Sergeant Frank Hawkrigg had learned more than a thing or two about life while he'd served on the front line – and his missing arm and leg bore witness to his education.

Yet his right hand waved in acknowledgement, the crowd could see as the open-top car progressed, and the smile he'd been known for around the village remained, except for the absence of a few teeth and the addition of a certain shadow.

The war hadn't left Ambleside alone – several men had already lost their lives in France, and the town continued to do what it could for the refugees who'd arrived over the past months. Yet seeing the ugly truth of battle, literally face to face, was altogether different.

The mayor, sat beside Hawkrigg in the car, did the standing up instead as they reached the market cross, and rolled into a parking position where those uphill could see their hero's back, while those below could only see the mayor.

There were still low cries of shock and dismay as more and more people began to sense, rather than see, the experiences the soldier had brought home. No one paid much attention to the mayor's speech. And they flinched and pitched in imitation of Hawkrigg's struggle to balance in an upright position. He couldn't wave while he used his one hand to steady himself on the back of the car, his half-leg bent back on the seat for more balance. But he could smile, and he did, beaming round the square like a second sun. 'By heck, it's grand to be home!' he shouted, and the cheering response was heartfelt.

Silence fell again as the mayor's entourage called for attention. 'I left the lads still fighting,' Hawkrigg went on. 'Hems is a sergeant now, like me, and Lamb and Flitters, they're making a bit on the side like always – and as for Hindmoor! Well, I can't tell you in the street, can I?' The crowd laughed, enthralled, but the mood moved as the hero's smile ever so slightly changed.

'We're going to carry on, and we're going to win,' he said more quietly, and more slowly, although his voice still carried. 'And do you know why? For this. For us. For Ambleside.

'Do you know what kept me going?' He seemed to have become an expert in telling stories, as he judged his pitch and pace with the precision of a military march. 'I've had this... discussion, you might say, for as long as I can remember, with Fred Stanley in the Golden Rule.'

A mutter of appreciation went round the square – Hawkrigg and Stanley's constant bickering had been a valued piece of entertainment in the pub. Despite their age difference, they'd taken to each other immediately, although they'd never admitted so, and no one thought they ever would. Instead they'd stood at opposite ends of the bar; Stanley, in his sixties, near the hatch, and Hawkrigg at the other end. Almost every night until the war came they'd argued over everything. And each night the argument ended with whether slate or sandstone was the best building material in the Lakes – with each arguing for the other, and neither knowing anything about building.

The soldier told the crowd: 'Do you know, every time things were tough, and they were, and every time things got a bit difficult to deal with, I'd picture myself, standing at the bar in the Rule, telling Fred Stanley he were bloody well wrong!'

As the crowd laughed again, the mayor leaned over and whispered something, a grim look on his face. 'Well,' Hawkrigg said loudly, 'Seems like that's not right talk for someone who's done his best.' His listeners glared at the politician, who smiled awkwardly. 'So I'll say no more!'

With a movement that belied his injuries, he threw himself over the side of the car and into the arms of the nearest villagers. One even had the presence of mind to grab his crutch from beside the mayor – and it, along with its owner, was soon lost in the throng. Alone in the car, embarrassed over the people's delighted response, the worthy waved for the band to strike up once again, and tried to recompose himself to suggest, with one studied look, that everything had happened the way he'd planned it.

Beyond the square a small group of people laughed long and loud as they made their way up North Road, past the Unicorn and round onto Smithy Brow. Outside the Rule, Hawkrigg pushed through those who had assisted with his escape, telling them: 'I'd best go in first.'

The pub was peaceful. A barmaid he didn't recognise attended to cleaning duties while nothing else moved – including Stanley, who leaned stock-still against the bar, back to the door, in his time-honoured place.

The barmaid responded to the sound of the soldier's crutch on the flagstones, and nodded when he said: 'Pint of mild, please.' His companions made as little noise as possible behind him, waiting for the hero to decide his move.

Stanley lifted his glass to his mouth, without looking round. 'It's bloody slate,' he said.

'It's bloody sandstone,' replied Hawkrigg, 'And the bloody drinks are on you.'

WELCOME TO THE FAMILY
Monday, February 14, 1921

TOM WHITEHEAD WASN'T GOING to let Briggs off the hook easily – he felt his point was valid. 'Just tell him all of that stuff,' the regular insisted.

'He's not going to care, is he?' the landlord insisted back. 'He's a brewery man. He cares about what makes money for the brewery.

He's not bothered about anything else.'

'Well, make him bothered!' Whitehead said. 'There's a reason this place was worth buying. Let him learn that, if he wants it to be worth keeping, he'd best leave best alone.'

The Hartleys man was expected any moment. The transaction had been completed two days previously – Mr Collins and Mr James, until recently owners of the Golden Rule, had sold it to the Ulverston brewing company, and the pub had become part of a chain. All that remained was to find out what it meant to those who frequented the premises; and, of course, those who found employment in it.

'Would you leave him be?' Harold Vity asked Whitehead. 'Poor man don't know if he's got a job tomorrow!'

'I'll be alright,' Briggs said loudly, although he wasn't as certain as he sounded.

A small, quiet-looking man in a loose suit came through the front door, put down his business bag, took off his glasses and rubbed his nose. He peered round the taproom as the patrons peered back at him. 'Mr Strickland?' Briggs asked.

The newcomer offered a narrow smile, moved to the bar and shook the landlord's hand. 'Welcome to the Hartleys family, Mr Briggs,' he said. 'I've just come for a bit of a look-round, if you don't mind. There's nothing to worry about.'

Whitehead cleared his throat, and everyone took his meaning. 'Been fine enough for two hundred year,' he said to Vity, at the other end of the bar, with Strickland between them.

'Aye,' Vity replied. 'And a grand history an'all. Poets, painters, balls, hunts – and forty years of legal meetings held here, inquests and all that.'

'Mentioned in a poem in 1842,' Whitehead added. A severe glare from Briggs stopped him going any further, and he decided to change the subject. 'Anyway, Harold, did you hear about Doug

Jennings catching that robber at the White Lion?'

'He never!'

'He did. Some flash-harry, neat as you like, got in behind the bar and got his hands on the takings, and ran for it...'

Briggs invited Strickland to step behind the bar. But after a moment of peering at the construction, and its row of pumps, he refused, and instead stepped slowly and cautiously into the lower sitting-room. 'Leave well alone,' Briggs whispered as he came through the hatch and followed the visitor down.

'Aye, so he's out of the Lion before anyone even knows what's happened,' Whitehead went on. 'Except Doug, he sees it all, so he goes out after the fella...'

Briggs didn't know what to say, but he assumed (he had to) that Strickland knew his business. The small man poked about around the fireplace, ran his fingers along the windowsills, stared at the ceiling, stared at the floor, stared at the furniture then stared at Briggs. He took out a notebook from his jacket pocket and began scribbling in it. Then he made an 'hm-hm' sound like a doctor might, and went back up the stairs and into the back sitting room.

'Now it just so happens that there were two constables outside the Lion. But of course, all they saw were one man running and another man chasing...'

Strickland repeated his performance in the back room, then again in the top sitting room, making sounds of additional interest as he examined the hatch once used for serving 'undesirables' who weren't allowed to drink on the premises.

'Doug got to him first, you see, put him on the floor and started knocking him about. He were bloody lucky the constables were there...'

Briggs followed Strickland through the back door into the yard, where they examined the stables, the beer cellar and the outhouses, and looked up at the wooden bridge that led to Newell's joinery workshop above the barn. Then they re-entered the pub by the private door, came through the kitchen and back into the bar and then upstairs.

'So they arrested the robber, but when they searched him they didn't find anything on him. What they didn't know was that Doug had already had the money off him...'

Strickland continued making notes as he went round the guest rooms and function room, then the staff premises on the floor above. Finally he snapped his notebook closed, offered Briggs a half-smile and began making his way downstairs.

'So Doug handed the money to Sally behind the bar, but the constables asked for it back before she put it away. Turns out there was twelve shillings missing, so they took the robber away to ask him about it...'

Briggs, and several of the regulars, watched Strickland as he took a piece of paper from his case, read over it and added something to the bottom. 'Then what happened?' he asked Whitehead.

The regular looked surprised. 'Well,' he said after a pause, 'it just so happened that twelve shillings were what Doug owed on his tab, and he paid it the next morning, though he'd been broke for the past month.'

Strickland laughed. 'What did they say at the White Lion?'

'What could they say?' Whitehead replied. 'He'd done them a favour. They had to do him one back, if they liked it or not!'

'I do like a good drinking pub,' Strickland said to Briggs. 'And this is a good drinking pub. Nothing to worry about here.'

CLARK'S LEAP

Tuesday, May 10, 1921

...And he caught his wife messing around, and not for the first time, and he'd had enough, and he decided to end himself. Not her, mind, himself, and he told her so. 'How are you going to do it?' she says. 'I'm going to hang myself,' he says.

But she tells him, 'It's more difficult than it looks, that hanging, and there's many a poor soul that doesn't quite finish the job, and just hangs there half dead and half alive.' So that talks him out of that.

Next he says, 'Well, I'll shoot myself, then.' She says, 'It's the same thing – if you're not a good shot, and you're not, how can you be sure you won't just hurt yourself and lie in pain for hours?' So he's not doing that neither.

Then he says, 'Well, how about drowning, then? How hard is that?' And she tells him, 'It's alright, as long as you take a good jump into the water, so it's nice and deep, and you don't wind up flapping your way back to the land, and take hours to die.'

So he goes, 'That's it, I'll drown myself, and take a good long jump.'

And he does just that – he takes a good long run and he drowns himself. Just the far side of the Swirls Gate, out Helvellyn way, you know where I am? It's called Clark's Leap, on account of his name were Clark, or he were a clerk. I don't remember.

Anyway, she, the widow, goes about her business, telling anyone and everyone as will listen that she did right by her husband till the day he died.

And that, since you asked, is why I worship my wife – I worship the ground that's bloody coming to her...

AMBLESIDE 93

Sunday, June 29, 1924

Hello, Tom – mind if I use the telephone?

You'll have to wait, Alan. There's a bit of a queue.

There always is! Best have a drink while I'm waiting. The usual, please. Here, it's good for your business, isn't it? Are most of us waiting to make a call?

Aye – and you're all having a drink or two while you do. To think someone suggested I should be charging for the calls themselves. This is far more profitable! Best thing I've done in years, getting that in.

It's a remarkable thing, in't it? Of course, I don't understand it myself. I mean, how does it use them numbers to work out where the person you want to talk to is? And how do you tell a telephone what number it is?

Well, they tell you the number when they fit it.

Aye, but someone's got to tell the phone, haven't they?

It's beyond me. I'm just glad it works.

Aye. I don't think it'll catch on, mind, the telephone. I can't get my head around the idea of talking to someone who isn't there.

Some say it's easier when you've had a drink...

I wouldn't know – I've not had the chance to use it without having had a few while I'm waiting!

Maybe that's for the best.

It might well be. It's my daughter I'm always talking to, and she's always saying she's never heard me happier. It's good for her so it's good for me. She needn't know why...

END OF A CYCLE

Monday, September 1, 1930

Dear Sirs —

As a fellow publican I wish to bring attention to the last will and testament of Mr. Mark Atkinson, until lately keeper of The Kirkstone Pass Inn, Ambleside.

A respected member of the community, Mr. Atkinson requested that his remains be cremated, his ashes enclosed in a box, and buried upon Caudle Moor, facing the inn he ran so well.

I am pleased to report that his wishes in this regard will be carried out this coming weekend.

Mr. Atkinson also said in his will, to quote: 'It is my express wish that my son Ion shall desist from motor-cycling.'

I am able to bear witness to the fact that young Mr. Atkinson's navigation of The Struggle, between his late father's hostelry and my own, have given many patrons of both cause for concern.

I believe close examination of his vehicle, and the damage discovered thereon, will support those concerns.

It is my fervent hope, on behalf of the community, that Mr. Mark Atkinson's express wish will be observed.

Yours etc —

Thomas Johnston Briggs, keeper,
The Golden Rule Inn, Ambleside

THE WRONG RACE
Thursday, December 1, 1932

GEORGE HODGSON threw his brand-new MG J2 Midget across the Clappersgate bridge, taking the racing line through the slow-right turn up the hill and onto Rothay Road, saving another few vital seconds as he finally settled on the legal side of the road.

He'd only had a few at Barngates so he felt in fine fettle as he pushed the straight-four engine towards its official limit of sixty-five miles an hour. The big houses on his left fell into shadow as the sun left off its hold over the fields on his right. The half-elliptic suspension bounced sharply as the cable-controlled brakes objected to his heavy touch – but only for a moment. He still had to reach, and top, sixty-five. The legal time was eleven minutes; he'd done it in eight, and he was aiming for seven.

The long slow left gave way to a middling right; then, at last, enough straight to touch the limit – sixty-six, sixty-seven, a drop for the medium left, one more kick, then the steep right for Rothay Bridge, passing the Ambleside road sign. Four and a half minutes gone.

The Hartford shocks did their job as the MG flew over the bridge and banked right. The power of eight hundred and forty seven horses gave their all via eight crossflow cylinders, two carburettors and fourth forward gear.

But he was no longer alone – in the dash-mounted mirror he could see PC Harper's Triumph NT giving chase, the policeman bent low over his handlebars.

'Come on, Dickie!' Hodgson shouted over his shoulder. 'Let's see what you've got!' It might just be enough: five hundred horses, twin-port overhead valve engine, three-speed gearbox, but just two wheels.

Of course, neither of them could hope to match the power of Sir

Malcolm Campbell's latest *Blue Bird*. They'd seen it together on British Pathe News the previous weekend – Rolls-Royce R-type V engine generating over two thousand horse power, expected top speed over two hundred and seventy. Campbell would be lucky to keep it on the ground.

Hodgson raced on. It was the best two hundred pounds he'd ever spent – that, and the twelve more for the temperature gauge, eight-day clock, mesh grilles and leather bonnet strap. And what a shade of green!

A steep left. One last chance to open her up as Harper closed behind him. Sixty-seven, sixty-eight, sixty-nine, five minutes forty seconds. Long slow right, long slow left and – at last! – into Ambleside and racing past Rothay Park.

Decision time, with just over a minute to go. Hodgson chose the left and right into Compston Road; there might be more pedestrians that way, but there were fewer steep turns to get back to the Rule. He threw a hand up in salute to Harper behind him: 'Well done, Dickie!' as their traditional splitting-point passed. But the bike kept coming.

He relied on the noise to warn passers-by, keeping him above a respectable fifty-five; but then, made a small mistake just before the steep-left into Rydal Road – his foot slipped from the accelerator, and, concentration broken, he mis-steered slightly. Alright, he might have had more than a few at Barngates. Still, it gave PC Harper a fighting chance.

One last bolt past Bridge House then all eight of the MG's brake drums screamed through the hard-right onto Smithy Brow. Another wave for Harper as Hodgson disappeared up the hill, a fast right followed by another one – the well-practised race into the yard behind the Rule. Seven minutes forty.

Hodgson leaned over, pulled the key from the ignition, sat back and laughed. Not quite what he'd aimed for – but not far off either. The Marles steering gear probably needed a small rake adjustment.

Stepping out of the car was like coming back to earth. At once the silence of the evening crashed down like a gear-change. He hoped there was someone in the pub who'd share his excitement.

He entered through the private door, leading through the kitchen to the bar. 'My landlord and host! I thought I heard you coming up the hill!' said Harper from the other side, lifting a near-empty glass in welcome.

Hodgson grinned. 'A good race!' He took the constable's glass to refill it, and reached for an empty one for himself. 'How did you beat me in? And parking outside isn't allowed!'

'What?' Harper laughed. 'I've been here since three. Off tonight. And hoping to enjoy it, if you'd be so kind.' He nodded towards the glass, which Hodgson had forgotten about.

'That's strange,' the innkeeper said, his lips pursed in doubt.

The side door opened. A shadow fell across the hallway. A tall police constable in motorcycle gear entered, and moved slowly, threateningly, towards Hodgson.

'Good evening, sir,' said the officer in his most official voice. 'Are you the owner of the green MG parked out the back?'

Harper turned away, his hand over his face.

THE CENTENARIAN
Wednesday, June 24, 1936

THE GRAND OLD LADY OF THE RULE was placed by the fire in the lower sitting room, where everyone could see her. No fewer than five generations of her family swirled around her while the newspaperman took notes as she spoke.

'I did indeed fall down them stairs," she said with a high, precise voice. 'It were three year ago. Fractured my head, I did. The doctors said I made a "remarkable recovery." She nodded for emphasis. '"Remarkable recovery," thcy said, for a woman of ninety-seven.'

The reporter shook his head. 'And I hear you had your hair bobbed for the first time last year?'

'I did!' she said proudly. 'You're never too old to try something new – just remember that.'

'And is there a secret to reaching a hundred years old?'

'Not as such,' she replied after a pause. 'Just keep going, and don't die!'

'Thank you so much, Mrs Holdsworth,' the journalist said, shaking her hand. 'It was a real pleasure!'

'You're welcome!' Ann told him, nodding and smiling as he left – until the moment he was out of sight. 'Thank God that's over!' she said in a completely different, more piercing and demanding voice. Hodgson – I'll have a pint!'

George had been waiting for the summons. It came regularly, and had done for the several years in which his mother-in-law had been living in the Rule. He used to believe it would end one day. Now he only hoped it might. 'Here you are, Ann,' he told her.

She didn't thank him. 'Of course, they'd never print what I really wanted to say,' she announced to no one in particular. 'Although you would think that, being a century old, you could say what you liked. Not that I do.'

'Of course not,' George said, because she happened to be glaring at him as she spoke.

'Of course not,' she agreed. 'And what would I have said?'

'Anything you like, Ann.'

'Aye, Anything about that Allenby.'

That old chestnut, George said in his head, and knew she knew what he'd though.

'That creature! Fraud! Thief! Brought my daughter and her man to near ruin, he did! I'll find him. One of these days, I'll find him.'

Ellis Allenby hadn't been heard of in over two years. The former owner of the inn, who'd found himself in financial trouble on a number of occasions, and in court nearly as many times, was probably on the other side of the world. He'd run off owing ninety pounds, and it was later discovered he owed four hundred to partners in a previous business – this after taking a large deposit for a hotel, then refusing to return it when the sale fell through.

'Does that reporter really want to know what keeps me going?' Ann shouted, as the five generations of her family let her get on with it. 'It's the desire to find Allenby and make him pay. I'll live as long as I must to find him!'

'And when she does, I can testify to the hell he'll be put through,' George told a regular quietly as he returned to the bar. 'Bloody old battleaxe.'

'Hodgson! Another pint!'

'Coming, Ann.'

HURRICANES DOWN

Thursday, August 14, 1941

CAPSTICK STARED INTO HIS PINT POT. 'It's a sad, sad thing,' he said, his drawn tone made hollow by the container. 'Two good men gone like that, and one a war hero.'

'Are you sure that's right?' said Nora, the landlady. 'I've not seen anything in the papers.'

'And you won't, neither. They don't put stuff like that in the paper. Operational secrets. Same reason all the road signs are down.'

'So how are we meant to know?'

'We're *not!*' Capstick frowned. 'They don't want anyone told anything that might affect morale. If this pub were bombed tonight, there'd be a story about a fire in the papers in a few days time, just for those who saw what happened, then nowt.'

Nora tutted. 'Well, what's the point of the papers then?'

'Morale! We live on a bloody island. The only thing that keeps us going is our determination. They know that, so they try and keep morale up.'

'If the papers aren't going to tell the news, I don't see the point. And if it's not in the newspapers, it didn't happen.'

'You tell that to the lads who climbed Scafell to collect the bodies. My lad were one of them. Two Hurricanes, two pilots dead, and one of them had a DFM for the Battle of Britain.'

'I don't believe it,' Nora said, waving her hand. 'What does a war hero want with a training flight?'

'They've got to keep their hours up,' Capstick said impatiently. 'They never know when they'll be needed. They can't sit about, forgetting how to fly just when they're needed.' He sighed as Nora topped his drink up. 'You see, they spotted the Lake District as training space about ten year ago – but no one thought to check the finer details. There's places where the wind moves against you, and if you get caught up in that, you're a goner. They should have done more checking.'

'Did you say ten years ago?' Nora frowned.

'Aye. Maybe longer.'

'But they didn't know there was going to be a war ten years ago!'

Capstick put down his drink and open his arms wide. '*Of course they did!*' he bellowed.

'How could they?'

'Give over, woman – it's been brewing up since the last war! Everyone knew it!'

'Well, I didn't!'

'Well, there you go then.'

'I didn't read anything about it anywhere.'

'There was plenty to read about it if you looked.'

'That's near treason, what you're saying.' Nora shook her head and moved away, while Capstick stared into his pot again.

'A sad, sad thing,' he said again, and his voice echoed through the pot and around the quiet taproom.

'We'll finish it this time, though, won't we, Albert?' young Gregg said from the corner.

'Aye, we will!' Capstick said with more confidence than he felt.

PASSING SHADOW
Friday, October 23, 1942

MINNIE FAULKNER HAD ENJOYED some success with what she called her 'grand plan' – her aim of making sure the regulars of the Rule mixed with the students of the Royal College of Art.

There had been much resentment when several dozen 'bright young things' had arrived to seek shelter from the London blitz, their world of painting, pottery and fabric work completely at odds with the Lakeland world of farming, mining and labouring.

Yet Minnie had been determined, in the spirit of all being in the war together, to bring the parties together. And the landlady didn't mind being pointed about it either. That's why Leslie Duxbury, Bill Kempster and their friends had been told to sit by the fire in the lower sitting room, and leave George Dawson where he was nearby.

'But Minnie!' Duxbury had said. 'Of all the people! George is a fine man, I'm sure, but he's so — so... George!'

'Sit there or don't sit at all,' she'd replied firmly.

The student had appealed to her husband Piggy (so-called because he kept pigs in the inn's back yard) but he knew better than to interfere with Minnie's grand plan. So the bright young things had taken their drinks and settled near the gruff old farmer, who said nothing as he watched them talk, perhaps emitting the odd grumping sound now and again.

'Steady on, love,' Piggy whispered. 'George in't exactly known for his friendly manner, is he? Remember last time one of them young folks tried to talk to him... he was lucky you didn't bar him after that.'

'Best stay out of it, Albert,' she told him. 'I've had a word with him.' (Piggy wasn't surprised.) 'We'll see what we'll see.'

Bill Kempster was displaying a pencil sketch he'd recently done, holding up the large piece of paper so his colleagues could see the image of a chair and table against a large window. 'It's not exactly adventurous,' he admitted, 'but I'm trying a little trick with the contrast, you see? Only, there's something wrong with it.'

'There is, isn't there?' Duxbury mused. 'Only, what?'

Several students squinted at the paper, moving their heads like a flock of sparrows watching a hawk. No one could identify the problem, but they all accepted there was one.

'What do you think, George?' Minnie said loudly from the top step.

'Think I want another drink,' the farmer replied sharply.

'I offered you one – you said you'd get it later,' Piggy told him.

'It's later now, innit?'

'You come and get it then,' Minnie said, 'And take a look at Bill's sketch.'

Dawson grumbled to himself as he made a performance of getting up, and shambled his large form past the fireplace. Doubtfully, Kempster made sure he could see the sketch, although he didn't go so far as to offer a close-up view. 'There's something not right,' he said awkwardly, aware that the farmer was already technically supposed to be involved in the conversation.

'Shadow under chair's wrong, innit?' Dawson said immediately. 'Going the wrong way.'

The students clustered round for another look. 'I think he's right,' Duxbury said with surprise. 'He is!'

Dawson pulled out a pencil from his pocket. 'Do you mind?'

'No,' Kempster said. 'It's only a sketch.'

Dawson leaned in and made just a few adjustments. 'Got to think about where light's going to as well as coming from,' he said quietly, with none of the usual gruffness. 'You got big windows there, so that changes your angle.' He stood up. 'That's it, innit?'

The students looked at his work, and agreed that it very much was it. 'Reckon you owe me a drink,' said the farmer, and made a noise which they realised was a laugh.

'Reckon I do,' Kempster said, while Minnie nodded at Piggy with satisfaction.

BOHEMIAN FAREWELL

Saturday, July 28, 1945

Dear Sirs —

It is with much gratitude and no little sadness that the Royal College of Art takes its leave of Ambleside this week.

There is no novelty in observing that much has changed in the world since the college arrived in exile at the beginning of the war. Yet it should be noted that, in the particular instance of the worldly-unwise students and the welcoming souls of this town, much has changed for the better as a result of their interaction.

As the months passed, there flowered a genuine mutual appreciation between the different parties, and finally, a strong interaction. We have been delighted to see postmen posing for sculptures and barmaids walking for fashion displays, while not a few of our students have learned the ways of milking, grooming and even roofing.

It was sadly predictable that the general election would reinforce many of the differences between the college and the town, with most of the students voting for Attlee and most of the citizens voting for Churchill, each and all with strongly-held beliefs to back their positions.

Yet we hope the differences will not be the lasting memory of these recent years; and that, instead, we will take a little of Ambleside with us when we go, and that we will leave a little of ourselves here.

We extend a warm invitation to join us in the Golden Rule on Thursday next, before our departure the next morning.

Yours sincerely

The staff of the Royal College of Art, billeted with pride in Ambleside, 1939–1945.

GETTING BETTER
Tuesday, August 12, 1947

YOU COULD ALWAYS TELL the ones who stumbled into the Rule and immediately realised they'd found a home from home – and often immediately began changing their plans for the rest of the day. But then, you could also tell the ones who knew they'd made a terrible mistake, and that marching straight through to the other exit would only compound it.

The two tall Londoners, with unaccountably loud voices, were of the second type. It took them moments to understand that the Rule wasn't their kind of place, and a few more moments to understand (without discussion) that they'd better have a half before moving on.

Victor Bennett bid them welcome, and, taking their order, served two half-pints of mild. He had a great deal of sympathy for them – because he suspected he was one of them.

'Have you come far, gents?' he asked.

'London,' came the reply from the taller man.

'Walking holiday?'

'No. We're here to meet Kurt Schwitters, as it happens.'

'Ah – artists!' Bennett said.

'No, journalists, actually.'

'I see! Well, you don't have far to go. You'll find Mr Schwitters just down the hill and round the corner, at Bridge House.'

He wished he could go with them, and leave the Rule behind. He'd admitted several weeks ago that it had been a mistake to take the place on. Nothing good had come of it, and he'd already taken steps to remedy it.

'Ah, yes, Bridge House,' said the smaller man. 'We went past it earlier on. We didn't see Schwitters there.'

'That's strange. He's there most days. He'd be almost certain to be there on a day like this, sun blazing down, tourists out. He draws them, you see.'

One of the visitors nearly spat out his drink. 'Kurt Schwitters? Sketching tourists? No.'

'He does. Sits at Bridge House and he'll draw anyone for a shilling or two.'

The taller one laughed. 'Schwitters is one of the leading lights of modern art,' he told Bennett, with no little disdain in his voice. 'I can't imagine what he'd be doing sketching tourists.'

'Perhaps,' the innkeeper replied evenly, 'He's learning to be an even better artist.'

The visitors finished their drinks and left without another word. Bennett was glad to see them go – and realised he was glad to be staying. The Rule had done something good for him after all.

FORGOTTEN JOHN

Thursday, January 7, 1954

OLD JOHN'S SEAT had been carried outside the pub, because that's where Old John wanted it. For more years than anyone could remember, it had been to the right of the fire, where Old John sat as often as he cared to, and others moved out the way each time.

Tall Alan came down the hill from The Struggle, and stopped for a moment by Old John on his seat. 'Why are you out here?' he asked. 'There's snow on the tops – you'll catch your death!'

'Already caught it,' Old John replied, sipping his ale.

Hillsides Pete came out of the door as Tall Alan went in. 'You should move indoors, John. This is no night to be outside.'

'It is for the one as I'm waiting for,' Old John said.

Young Alfie came up Smithy Brow from the road to Grasmere. 'Come on inside, John,' he said. 'It's going to be a cold one tonight.'

'Colder for me,' Old John replied. 'I'll soon be following you along that road – in a coffin.'

Inside the pub, the row of regulars stood facing the wall behind the bar. 'You can't tell him anything at his age,' said Big Martin. 'He knows it all.'

'Happen he does,' Butcher Sid agreed. 'When you've lived the years and worked the days he has, you're entitled to say and do as you want.'

'What age is he, anyway?' Alfie asked.

'Eighty-eight,' said a regular.

'Ninety four,' said another.

'Hundred and two, I make it,' said a third.

'God knows,' sighed a fourth.

'That's just what's getting to him,' Sid announced. 'He thinks God doesn't know. Thinks God's forgotten him.'

'I'm going to get him in,' Alfie said.

'Might as well take him this,' Tall Alan told him, handing over a fresh pot of ale.

Outside the temperature had dropped noticeably. There was frost in the high skies and the snow-covered hilltops glowed in silver-blue moonlight, while the first rolls of fog began to billow down The Struggle from Kirkstone.

Alfie waited while Old John finished his ale, then took the empty from him and replaced it with the full. 'You need to come in, John. God knows how cold it's going to get.'

'There's a lot of things God knows, and a lot of things he seems to have forgotten,' John replied after a moment. 'Like me. Here I am, older than the lot of you, and still working my days better than a lot of you. Langholm's gone, Fazakerley's gone, Sandy's gone, my old wife... It's my turn tonight.'

'Don't talk like that!' Alfie said sharply.

'I'll do as I please, at my age,' Old John muttered. 'There's plenty of you and your type have told me how to behave, and I've seen you all off. But I've had enough. So, tonight —' he opened his scarf a little, as if to speed up the process — 'Tonight, I'm sitting out here till God remembers me, and takes me with him.'

'As if he'd have you,' Alfie said quietly, and received a non-committal grumble in response.

'I was going to hand in my notice in the morning,' the old man continued. 'Hand in my cards. Then I thought, 'Why bother? Let God do it. He owes me that at least, doesn't he?"

Alfie sighed and went back inside. 'Says God will take him tonight,' he told the regulars. 'Opened his scarf up, he did, to let the cold in. Says he's sick of seeing everyone else to their graves. He was going to hand in his notice —'

'He's been saying that once a month since I met him forty years back,' Tall Alan bellowed.

'Well, this time he means it,' Alfie replied, then, more quietly, added: 'I really think he means it.'

'Born to work, that one,' Sid observed. 'Started when he was eleven, still doing dawn till dusk on the roads near a hundred years on.'

'Maybe God *has* forgotten him,' Alan suggested.

'Or maybe God's waiting for another who has the same good sense about hard work,' Sid said. 'There's not many. Him, and me.'

'Away!' Alan cried. 'You'll never make a hundred and whatever. You'll retire the first moment you can, with your sons to run the shop for you.'

Sid ignored him. 'Work then drop,' he said into his drink. 'There's many who'd call that a life well lived.'

'Well, not me,' Alfie said. 'I'm off to bring him in. I'll lift him if I have to. Sid, Alan, come on.' He marched to the door, and the others followed without complaint.

Outside it was colder still. Loughrigg to the west was lost in the fog, with little points of yellow light from the houses on Smithy Brow fading into the ice clouds, which crawled over from above and behind, slowly blotting out the moonlit snow.

And Old John's seat was empty – except for the ale pot.

'He's gone!' Alfie said. 'It's... happened!'

'Do you think...?' Alan whispered. 'Do you really think...?'

'Don't be daft!' Sid bellowed. 'God doesn't take you like that!'

'Someone else might,' Alan said darkly.

'Now don't you — look!' Sid abandoned his argument as he pointed up the hill, where the vague pillar of a shadow appeared to be moving, slowly, away from them. Its shape billowed and wove, lit from a streetlight behind, as the freezing fog rolled around it.

'John! John!' Sid shouted. 'Is that you, John?'

The shadow took a different form – it thinned, then vanished, then grew wider, and suddenly taller. 'Aye, it's me!' came a muffled voice wrapped in the depth of night.

'Are you... are you all right?' cried Sid.

'I am that!' Old John shouted. 'I can't be sitting drinking with you all night –– I'm up for work in the morning! Good night!'

He vanished into the mist. Alfie picked up the pot and Danny picked up the seat, while Tall Alan held the door open, and the three went back inside.

WAINWRIGHT'S VISIT

Thursday, May 22, 1969

THE BIG MAN SEEMED to be trying to disappear into his corner, using his glasses, the table and lunch before him as a disguise. On the surface he seemed calm and disinterested – but there was something about the way he held himself that suggested he was working incredibly hard to be left alone.

'Is that him?' Hardacre whispered, as if the man's aura of power extended as far as the bar.

'Aye, it is,' Dawson whispered back, before they both turned back to their drinks.

'Doesn't say much, does he?'

'Well, he writes it all, I suppose.'

'Wainwright.' Hardacre said the name slowly, as if two short syllables weren't enough to contain everything that the man in the corner represented.

It was indeed Alfred Wainwright, the man who'd hand-drawn every page of a seven-book guide to the Lake District. He'd become famous for it – and nearly as famous for the contradiction that, while he'd inspired thousands of people to visit the Lakes, he didn't want to talk to any single one of them.

'It's true what they say – keeps himself to himself,' Hardacre mused, glancing at the big man via the mirror behind the bar.

'He should have kept everything to himself,' Dawson replied. 'He's bloody ruined this place. Hillwalkers round every corner, tourists in every pub. He'd better not be writing about the Rule – last thing we need is a book about the Rule...'

Wainwright stood up and left, making very little noise for a person of his stature. Edgar Peake moved out from behind the bar to clear the table, and returned with the plate and cutlery in one hand, and a banknote in the other. 'He's left money for you two to have a drink on him,' the innkeeper said, eyebrows raised.

'Aye, well. Good on him,' Hardacre said.

'He's a grand man, is Wainwright,' Dawson agreed.

MEN ONLY

Tuesday, May 18, 1971

BARBARA WAS HAPPY TO ACCEPT that Jean had a point, only she wasn't sure there was any point going on about it so. But she offered her support as best she could: 'There's no two ways about it, Jean, you're right.'

'Of course I'm right,' her friend said. 'It's a lot of nonsense, having them in there and us out here. You'd think our money wasn't good enough.'

She was referring to the recent partition installed in the taproom, which meant the area around the fireplace was reserved for men only – and of a certain age and a certain regularity. Women weren't allowed in, young men were only allowed by invitation, and passing trade was distinctly frowned upon.

'Is anyone's money good enough these days, with this decimal-isation?' Barbara said, hoping to change the subject. 'I can't tell my shillings from my fivepences.'

'A shilling is a fivepence,' Jean replied, ignoring the fact that her friend had been joking. But she didn't remain on the topic. 'It's getting all too far in one way around here. Men only corner, boxing club out back. Whatever next?'

'They've got to find ways to bring more money in,' Barbara suggested. 'Now they don't take guests overnight. You should see that corner during the day – full of drivers from the Ribble bus company, looking for a bit of peace. They wouldn't come in if that corner weren't there.'

'Well, I'm not standing for it,' Jean said, her face set. 'I'm going to sit in there whether they like it or not.' She stood up.

'Oh, don't bother with it,' Barbara pleaded. 'You'll only get folk upset.'

'Maybe they should be!' her friend replied. 'Come on!' She lifted their drinks and stamped forward. Barbara was compelled to follow, then take the lead so she could deal with the doors.

The entrance door had once led straight into the taproom, but that route was now blocked, and visitors were obliged instead to use doors in the left and right walls of the vestibule. Barbara came out of the left door, which gave access to the taproom, stepped across the vestibule doubtfully, and opened the right door – into the men's room.

Inside, two bearded men played dominoes at a table while four bus drivers read newspapers, smoked and sipped beer. None of the six paid the women any attention. Jean looked round, crestfallen, then turned back to the taproom door.

'Nothing to see there except old men,' she said when they'd returned to their places.

'It won't last,' Barbara said.

'No,' Jean replied, then laughed. 'I've just thought of something!'

'What?'

'You know how the Golden Rule is to be listed as a protected building, seeing as it's so old?'

'Aye?'

'And you know those Russian dolls, when you open one up and there's a smaller one inside?'

'Aye.'

'Well, that's like their men's room, isn't it? You open this big relic of a building and there's all those little relics in there!'

MAMMY DUGDALE'S SECRET
Wednesday, March 14, 1973

The old witch of Church Street – what was her name, Harry?

Mammy... Dugdale.

Mammy Dugdale! Aye, that were her. Old witch.

She weren't that old. She just looked it.

Sign of a witch, that, in't it? Looking old when you're not.

Sign of a wife an'all.

But you remember her clag'em? You must remember Mammy Dugdale's Clag'em.

What, the sweet?

Aye! The mint sweet, that she made in that big cauldron at the back of her shop.

Cauldron – there's another sign of a witch.

Aye, but her clag'em. Great stuff! Big long stretch of minty stuff, pulled out then cut into little bits. Who didn't break a tooth on it?

Didn't she pass the recipe on when she died?

She did that – but whoever it was couldn't make it right. It were never the same. They say it's because she spat in it, and on one else could spit like Mammy Dugdale.

That's it, gone now, then.

Same as the tree that used to be in Church Street.

Aye.

SOME FOR THE ROAD
Saturday, March 21, 1981

THE BIG SCOTSMAN had been visiting for long enough that everyone knew what he drank, and that he drank it from an old-fashioned pint pot. He'd introduce the concept by telling those who didn't know that he used to have his own pot hanging on a peg in a pub in Glasgow, but the pub was gone, although he still had the pot.

'And the best thing about them,' he'd tell anyone and everyone, 'Is that, once it's empty, you can smash it off someone's face if they've been bothering you – then hand it back over and say, 'Fill it up again!" Everyone assumed, or at least hoped, he was joking.

He often had what he called a 'drouth' on him, which meant his short but bulky frame absorbed as many as five pints in an hour, and on occasion, seven. But he didn't cause much trouble, and took himself off when it was time. He preferred to stand at the hatch end of the bar, but moved if a regular came in; so on the whole he was a good customer.

The four men at the corner table were also tourists, but it was their first visit. In truth they considered themselves lucky to be in the pub at all, because they'd only arrived with their families that evening. The relatively small kitchen had led the wives to decide that dinner would be made more easily in their absence, so they'd been given permission to have a couple of halfs, as long as they were back in the cottage by eight.

'He's had another one!' whispered one of the men – although the part of southern England he came from meant it was a whisper everyone could hear. 'How many's that?'

'I don't know,' said one of his companions. 'But we've had three halfs in just under an hour and a half, and he's had at least six pints.'

'It's almost... admirable!' another said, and the four men nodded slowly, no longer hiding their fascination as the Scotsman waved his empty pot at the barman, nodded towards it and grinned as it was refilled.

'We'd better go,' said the fourth. 'It's nearly eight.'

'I want to see if he has another,' the first replied. 'Let's have one more half, and we'll tell the women we lost track of time.'

'They probably expect that, don't they?' said the third, to which his companions agreed too quickly, sending him to the bar for four halfs as his punishment.

He couldn't resist the opportunity to stand beside the Scotsman as he waited to be served – although starting a conversation was a different idea completely. Finally, he ventured: 'Having a good night?'

The big one, who'd been staring into the pint that was already a third gone, seemed to be startled. He looked round, grinned, held up the glass and replied: 'Getting better every minute!'

That was enough risk for one conversation. Armed with the four halfs he returned to the table and took his seat, in time to overhear the Scotsman politely asking for another pint. 'Maybe change the glass this time, eh?' he asked the barman. 'Getting a bit foustie, I think.'

'That's another!' cried the visitor who'd given up any attempt at a whisper.

'It's almost like… a sport!' said another.

'I can't stop watching!' the third agreed.

'He's not even been to the toilet!' the fourth noted, almost aghast.

By the time the halves were downed, the man at the bar had begun yet another drink – and yet appeared no different in behaviour and stature than when they'd arrived.

It was time to go – but, encouraged by the warm reaction he'd had during the first encounter, the third visitor felt bold enough to engage again. 'Excuse me,' he said, tapping the Scotsman's shoulder, and stepping back a little just in case.

The other turned round, with that same near-regret at being distracted from his pint, quickly replaced by the apparent friendly grin. 'Aye!' he said.

'I'm sorry, but I really have to ask. We've been watching you for nearly two hours. How many drinks have you had?'

The Scotsman looked taken aback for a moment, and a dark look passed over his face, as if the question confused then angered him. But the notion was suddenly replaced by an infectious, almost smug, joy as he grinned his grin once more.

'*Some!*' he said brightly.

STEEP CLIMBS, HIGH SEAS

Monday, May 6, 1985

IT WASN'T VERY LIKELY that Albert Lamb could still focus on the newspaper on he table in front of him, but he continued the performance of reading it. His act of announcing interesting snippets – well, snippets that *he* found interesting – continued too, although there was a notable slurring in his voice.

'Are you climbers?' he asked two newcomers as they waited for John to pour their pints.

'Aye,' replied the smaller one, a short, gruff sort with grey hair and beard.

'Where have you been?' Albert asked.

'Dovetail Groove, out of Patterdale,' said the other, a taller, wirier man with bushier hair and beard, and a notably refined voice.

'I suppose that's quite adventurous,' Albert allowed, struggling with the long word. 'But if you want real adventure, you take a leaf from Geoffrey Waring's book.'

'Who?' the smaller one demanded.

'In here,' Albert replied, pointing at the paper. 'He's seventy-four year old and he's just joined rep theatre in New Zealand.'

The bearded men looked at each other, bewildered as to why they were being told. 'So?' said the smaller one.

'Geoffrey Waring were born in this pub,' Albert began. 'Back in nineteen-oh-nine, son of Charles, who were the landlord then. He always wanted to be an actor, did Geoffrey. Got his big break when he were just a lad – he were skating on ice at Rydal when a woman fell through, and he saved her, and she turned out to be a big-shot director from London, so she got him work.'

The men were still bewildered, but Albert was in full flow. 'Geoffrey Waring were one of the first people to appear on the BBC when it started. Then the war came along, and Geoffrey became a hero. He were captain of the Queen Mary when she were a troop transport, and she got attacked by a Jerry marauder. He couldn't turn guns in time, so he just rammed the Jerry. Saved everyone and got a medal.'

That had the visitors more interested, and Albert knew it, so he took a long pause, forcing the smaller man to demand: 'Well?'

'Well, he had a grand career as an actor, then he retired to New Zealand a few years back. But he got bored, so a few months back he went along to this theatre and told them he were only sixty, and they gave him job in *The Cherry Orchard*, that play by Chekhov. Rave reviews, he's getting – and he's seventy-four!'

'That's real adventure for you,' Albert finished, and went back to his paper. The bearded men looked at each other, took their drinks and sat down at the fire.

John came out from behind the bar and leaned over Albert. 'You get yourself into right trouble with your mouth, you do,' he said.

'What did I say? I only told them if they were looking for real adventure they wouldn't find it on that Horseshoe walk.'

'They didn't do the Horseshoe,' John said. 'They did Dovetail Groove. It's on the Horseshoe, but it's no walk. It's a real challenge.'

'Oh aye?'

'And they were only climbing that for old time's sake, because they were first to climb it,' John said quietly. 'Those two are Chris Bonington and Don Whillans. You don't get more adventurous than them. You daft old goat.'

THE GHOSTS OF MARDALE GREEN
Sunday, December 10, 1989

Alan, you've seen them, haven't you? The ghosts of Mardale Green.

Ah, they're not scary!

They are if you says it like this: The *ghoooosts* of *Maaardaaale Greeeen...*

They're not scary at all.

But you have seen them?

I have that. You can too, if you like. Any clear night when the moon's shining. Take yourself up there and you'll see them under Haweswater.

Ghosts under water?

Aye, because that's where Mardale Green is. They flooded the town, you see, back in nineteen thirty four or thereabouts, to raise the reservoir for Manchester. It's down there, some houses and a nice old church.

What about the people?

Well, they rehomed them, of course. Old Bertie Thomas, he came from Mardale Green. You can ask him when next he's in.

So who are the ghosts then, if there's no one there?

Must be folk buried in the churchyard, or whatever. I don't know – but I've seen them. Little lights under the water, moving about like they're walking up and and down the road.

It's not ghosts – it's the reflection of the moon! That's why you can only see them when the moon's out!

You go there then, watch out for them, and tell me it's the moon. I'll tell you now and I'll tell you then, it's not. It's just spirits going about their business. They're not scary. Unless there's a storm blowing when you're up there – the noise of them trees is more unhinged than any ghost...

You'll be telling me next the pub is haunted.

This building's near four hundred year old – of course it's haunted!

REGULAR ROUTINE

Sunday, February 24, 1991

THE VISITOR couldn't help but enjoy the display of traditions that were going on around him. When he'd arrived the Rule had been empty, except for a large man in a purple jumper, who sat quietly under the window. Placing himself at the bar, the visitor had started reading a Sunday paper, happy to enjoy the peace. But just before noon the pub had filled up over a matter of minutes, and it seemed that everybody but him was a regular.

'They come out of church, see, then come up here,' John explained from behind the bar as he worked his way through orders of beer, coffee, water and filled rolls. 'Busy as you like for two hours, then it calms down again at two. Oh-oh, here's trouble!'

The large man in the purple jumper moved slowly over from his place at the window. 'Feel free to buy a drink!' John said.

'Aye,' replied the large man.

'He don't say much,' John said to the visitor. 'And when he does, you soon realise he shouldn't!'

'Speak when I have to,' the large man answered, offering no hint that he was in any way offended.

'Go back and sit down – I'll bring it over,' John told him.

'Proper gent.'

'Not really. I just don't want your nonsense anywhere near me!'

'Just hurry up.'

John lifted a half-pint glass from its place beside the till, and waved it towards the visitor. 'This is his spending money,' he said. 'When it's gone, he's gone.'

'Everyone knows what's what.'

John poured a pint and took it over to the large man's table. 'He's a one-off, is this one,' he said over the noise of the room, still talking directly to the visitor. 'He once lost a truck. A flippin' great wagon loaded with trees, he was driving, and he parked it and lost it!'

'Easy done,' the large man said dismissively.

'Then there's that time he fell into the snow,' John continued as he went back behind the bar. 'Fell back off a wall into a great big drift, and when we found him he were still there, upside down, up to his ankles in snow!'

'I were quite comfortable,' the large man replied.

'And who could forget the bullock?' John said with a hand over his mouth for dramatic effect. 'There was once a slaughterman on the corner there, and they had a bullock escape. It ran into the back yard then into the toilets, and it wouldn't come out. They tried everything – they had the door off, they had the window off, but the thing couldn't be taken out. In the end they had to shoot it, in the toilet, and butcher it right there. And he —' John pointed over to the large man — 'Just sat in here while it all went on, wanting to know when his next drink was coming!'

'It were none of my business,' the large man said, standing up and putting on his coat. 'Nowt to do with me.'

'Where are you going?' John asked him.

'Home.'

'But you've still got money left!'

'I'll use it next time,' the large man said. 'Even a pig knows when he's had enough.'

THE GOLDEN RULE
Last night

LORD LOVE HIM, but he'd had enough to drink – and it wasn't just the staff who could tell.

But the young man had behaved impeccably since his first visit a few weeks ago. He'd observed all the understandings without having to be told. He'd made certain he wasn't taking anyone's place at the bar, and if he was, moved when they arrived. He'd only cautiously joined in the conversations, remaining on the outer edge and carefully measuring if and when it was appropriate to join in.

Put simply, he was going to be a perfect regular, and a great addition to the community. (Assuming, of course, he turned out to be as well-toned in character as he was in behaviour, but that was always the risk, and it was the pub's risk.)

Still, there was not getting round the fact that he'd had more than enough – although, because he was young, the drinker's greed for 'just one more' was on him. It was time to test that risk.

John moved towards the young man, who stood a little drooped at the door end of the bar, just where the pork pie sign, the charity boxes, the newspapers and the books for sale were kept. The other staff stepped back with respect, making no big deal of it, while the regulars, who'd gently built up a little distance from him, made a point of getting on with the conversation. It was an important moment and John had to be left to conduct it in his own manner.

'That'll be you for the night,' said John cheerfully, making it sound like a question even though it wasn't. The young man took it well and nodded, drinking the last of his pint. 'There's plenty more tomorrow, isn't there? And you've got to get up that bloody hill. Doesn't matter how long you've been here, it's still —' he made a rolling-eyed face of theatrical dread, raising a vague smile from the young man.

'Come on, lad.' The 'lad' was important, and the young man knew it, as John came out from behind the bar and gently led him to the door, pulling it wide open for him and ushering him outside.

No matter how pleasant a night, no matter how pleasant a visit, Ambleside is a different world from the Golden Rule. Thousands upon thousands of people have stepped through the door out onto Smithy Brow, wished they were going downhill, then looked up the steep road that, to this day, can become a river when the elements decide. And as the night air strikes, thousands upon thousands of people have realised that – even though they'd rather go back inside, with the fire warm, the lights bright, the beer fresh and dozens of conversations in full flow – it's the right decision to leave.

'Aye, plenty more tomorrow,' John said, patting the young man's back and offering an expression that casual visitors see but couldn't be expected to understand. 'And the night after, and after that an'all!' He laughed, with his hand over his face in a conspiratorial gesture.

'You get up that hill,' he said, moving the hand over the young man's shoulder and offering the other in a handshake. 'And you keep this in your head:

Call frequently
Drink moderately
Pay immediately
Be good company
Part friendly
Go home quietly.

'Just you respect that golden rule, and the Golden Rule will respect you.'

HISTORICAL NOTE

Each story in *The Rule Book* was sourced via a wide range of newspapers, books, archives and websites, which would need another book to list them. Every story either took place in the Rule, or was told to me at the bar. Many of the conversation-style stories are adjusted from discussions I overheard in the pub.

As always with historical fiction, a good deal of license has been taken in the interests of entertainment. There are also many basic facts which have been lost in piles of archives, and which proved impossible to recover within the timeframe of writing. I know some details of the changes within the Rule building over time, but it's not been easy to ascertain when they took place. Instead, I've worked within a relatively static layout, even though I'm aware it was never that simple. For uniformity's sake a similar approach has been taken to the physical development of Ambleside itself.

Most of the named licensees and staff really existed, and many of the other characters did too. All the fictional characters are based on people I've encountered at the bar, and I gave them their names from the war memorial at St Mary's church. It seemed somehow appropriate and I hope it doesn't offend anyone.

But nothing here is *entirely* fictional – and it all involved the Golden Rule in some way.

GOLDEN RULE TIMELINE

The following details were gathered from a number of archives including the Rule's own records, Robinsons Brewery, authority accounts and newspapers. All errors are my own.

1508: Richard Braithwaite (grandson of Robert, the first of the name to rise to prominence in Ambleside) begins extensive development of what will become known as Ambleside Hall

c1683: Ambleside Hall development ends; the part of the building to become the Golden Rule is then the brewery

1723: Part of the the estate, including Bridge House, is sold to John Benson, leaving the Braithwaite family via a 'complicated' will; it becomes known as Old Ambleside Hall as the Braithwaites build new premises on How Head

1738: John Benson listed as innkeeper in quarter sessions record

1791: Mary Armitt lists five hostelries in Ambleside – the Salutation, the White Lion, the Unicorn, the Fox And Goose and 'one unsigned'

1815: John Holme licensed as victualler in district record

1821: William Wilson named as licensee, with the name Golden Rule first noted; Estate auction of George Ellis held at Rule

1827: Inquest into death of Joseph Greaves held at Rule

1830: Death of John Barwise, leaseholder of Golden Rule Public House

1833: New Road opens below Smithy Brow, offering travellers the opportunity to enter Ambleside from the Grasmere direction without passing the Rule's front door

1835: John Holme's possessions, including the Golden Rule, auctioned off; Thomas Holme is already running the premises

1838: Ann Partridge, former housemaid at the Rule (employee of John Holme) kills herself and her five children; Thomas Harrison named as licensee; one of four town arches built at the Rule to celebrate the coronation of Queen Victoria; first mention of Golden Rule's annual sports day; Tithe Commutation Act meeting held in the pub

1839: Inquest into death of two-week-old child and watermill auction both held at Rule

1840: Two men convicted of stealing a candlestick from the Rule; admit being drunk, both fined 5s each

1841: Census reports Thomas Harrison, 35, as publican, along with wife Margaret, 43 and daughter Mary Ann, 20; plus a household that includes residents of dwellings in the back yard. George Newton, 29, named as owner

1842: Golden Rule mentioned in poem about local grandee's wedding celebrations; inquest into death of infant James Thompson held in pub

1844: William Black, licensee, fined 20s for selling alcohol to non-travellers on a Sunday; inquest into death of three-month-old child held at Rule

1845: Labourer John Jackson fined £1 for assaulting PC John Longmire in the Golden Rule

1846: Licensee William Black is expected to be fined £50, and lose his licence, for breaking Sunday trading law for third time – but punishment is held over

1847: Former licensee John Holme dies aged 76

1848: Ann Black, co-owner, fined 16s for slapping the face of resident James Hunter

1851: Juvenile ball runs until 3am; census lists household including William Black, 48, wife Ann, 43 and son George, 7, plus servant Mary Baker, 20 and three households in the back yard; George Newton remains as owner, living in Waterhead

1853: William Black, licensee, dies aged 54 'after a lingering and painful illness borne with exemplary patience' – license transferred to widow Ann Black

1855: License transferred from Ann Stainton, formerly Black, to new husband Robert Stainton, following their marriage in December 1854

1856: New licensee John Cowell's grocery burns down the night before he and his family move to the Rule; he loses stocks, cash and valuables, and was not insured

1857: Owner George Newton dies, leaving the Rule to his niece Victoria Mary, aged 8 (a sampler she embroidered this year is kept in the Armitt Museum)

1859: John Cowell forced to give up the Rule; applications invited for the let, while 'all the valuable, modern, household furniture, brewing vessels, bar utensils, stock in trade and effects' are sold at auction; Cowell's debtors paid one dividend; Matthew Harrison named as new licensee

1860: Ventriloquist charged for breaking a window after he threw stones at a private house, believing it to be a window of the Rule – he was trying to enter his lodgings late at night

1861: Harrison's two-year-old son Thomas dies; census lists household as containing Matthew (29); wife Jane (25); son James (1m); Daniel Gill, brewer (63); Sarah Millican, servant (23); and boarders Thomas and Mary Rothwell

1862: Inquest into death of labourer Edward Bell held at Rule

1866: "Spirited hunt" ends with grand gathering in the Rule; traditional "auld wife bake" runs from 6pm until 5am in the pub's ballroom

1863: inquest into drowning of tourist in Stock Ghyll Force held at Rule

1864: Inquest into drowning of four-year-old boy held at Rule

1867: Mrs Harrison donates a 'fat sheep' as a prize in the Fifth Westmorland Ambleside Volunteers' shooting contest (Mr Brown of Queen's Hotel gives forequarter of mutton as consolation prize)

1868: Last brewer listed on Rule census, Daniel Gill, dies aged 70 in September; Con-man arrested after fooling Rule owners and others into lending him money, giving him food, drink and clothes – claimed he was a seaman with £50 to spend and was waiting for his luggage to arrive with his cash

1871: Census – Matthew Harrison, innkeeper and farmer, 39; wife Jane, sons James, Benson, daughter Mary, brother Thomas, servants Alice Proctor, Elizabeth Nelson

1877: Owner Victoria Mary Newton entrusts her estate, including the Rule, to the use of Charles Collins and Joseph Hallawell; William Copley named as current tenant

1881: Census – William Copley, Innkeeper, 43; wife Hannah, son William Henry, servants Matthew B Harrison, Mary E Hutchinson; William Copley sues Miss Harriet Townson (Hill Top) for £26 for negligence in driving his cow over a garden wall, so that it fell 10ft and died – case found in favour of Ms Townson

1891: Census lists household as William Copley, 52; wife Ann, 41; servant Alice Whitehead, 16; plus three boarders and two family living in yard, now named Newalls Yard after resident Thomas Newall, a joiner

1897: Joseph Jackson named as licensee; owner Victoria Hallawell dies, leaving Charles Collins as trustee of estate, with Arthur James appointed as co-trustee

1901: Census – Joseph Jackson, 39, hotel keeper; wife Sarah, 44; daughter Maggie, 5; servant Crissie Hutchinson, 22, and groom James Gibson, 46; with the Newalls remaining in Newalls Yard and another family also in yard

1904: Joseph Jackson dies; his will entered into Cumbria records

1905: Mrs Mary Jackson named as proprietor

1906: Charles Henry Wearing named as licensee

1911: Census – Charles Henry Wearing, 39; wife Martha, children Henry, George and Geoffrey; servant Mary Jackson, her husband George (joiner). Geoffrey later becomes acclaimed actor, working well into his 80s

1916: Wearing offers 3-bedroom apartment for rent

1921: Golden Rule sold to Hartleys Brewery by Charles Collins and Arthur James

1923: J Wilson named as proprietor of Golden Rule Hotel, phone number Ambleside 93

1924: Thomas Johnson Briggs named as proprietor of Golden Rule Hotel

1931: Owner Thomas Ellis Allenby sued for the return of £45 after taking deposit for sale of Redwell Hotel then not returning it when sale was cancelled; Judge finds in Allenby's favour

1932: George Hodgson named as licensee; remains until 1940; bank of four hand pumps installed on bar, which will remain in service until 2014

1933: Ann Holdsworth (possibly mother-in-law of Hodgson) fractures her skull falling down the stairs in the Rule; makes a 'remarkable' recovery despite being 97

1934: Former owner Thomas Ellis Allenby is the subject of bankruptcy examination after losing £90 while owning the Rule, along with £420 in a previous business; number in phone book is Ambleside 184

1936: Ann Holdsworth celebrates her 100th birthday with a party, attended by five generations of her family; remains living the Rule with her daughter and son-in-law

1937: Ann Holdsworth dies two months short of her 101st birthday – 'She was married 77 years ago and had 18 children, five of whom are living. When Mrs Holdsworth was 98 she had her hair bobbed.'

1940: Students of the Royal College of Art, billeted in Ambleside after being evacuated from London, begin to frequent the Rule

1942: Albert Edward Faulkner named as licensee

1945: Arthur and Nora Bruce named as licensees

1946: Victor Emanuel Bennett named as licensee

1948: John Elleray named as licensee

1952: Daniel Smith named as licensee; the phrase 'Just a country inn' seen in promotional material

1954: Phone number listed as Ambleside 2257

1959: Annie Smith named as licensee

1963: Bill Tate named as licensee

1968: Edgar Peake named as licensee

1969: Ambleside Amateur Boxing Club starts in outbuilding; men-only section built in main bar, remains for a few years

1974: The building and its related group of houses is listed Grade II; around this time the Rule stops offering hotel accommodation

1975: Arthur Caterall named as licensee; Dave Oldham replaces him during the year

1981: John Lockley becomes licensee, remains until present day

1982: Hartleys taken over by Robinsons; the Rule is one of 56 pubs transferred to new ownership

2008: Boxing Club leaves premises

ALSO BY MARTIN PETER KIELTY

Highland Scotland, 1688: The forces of the deposed King James gear up for battle with those of the new King William – which is of little consequence to one Aberdeen beggar who is about to be murdered for sport.

Saved by one Simon Fraser of Beaufort, who calls himself 'The Young MacShimi,' the poor man is renamed Bolla after a Clan Fraser tradition, and finds himself embroiled in a world of war and intrigue.

Simon, seemingly a Jacobite, will stop at nothing to become chief of his clan. As those above him begin to be removed from his path, and he sets himself at odds with one of the most powerful families in the new Scotland, he earns himself the nickname 'The Fox.' Bolla can only bear witness as a chain of death and drama leads the Frasers to a dangerous, deadly reckoning...

Based on the real-life historical character Simon Fraser, 11th Lord Lovat – the last noble to be executed in British history.

'From the bloody snow of Glencoe to the blackened cellars of Edinburgh Castle and from the Bass Rock to the Battle of Killiecrankie, this is an epic tale of treachery, heroism, ambition and betrayal.'

~ DOUGLAS JACKSON, Hero Of Rome series

'Lechery, murder, rebellion and treachery – Simon Fraser of Lovat makes Flashman look like Noddy. Yet, somehow, Mr Kielty has contrived to make us love him too, while weaving a first-class story.'

~ ROBERT LOW, The Oathsworn series

Published by Sennachie Press   ISBN 978-1-326-10555-6   www.simonthefox.com